THE
PATERNITY
PUZZLE

AIMEE NICOLE WALKER

The Paternity Puzzle
(Sawyer and Royce: Felonies and Fatherhood Book One)

THE
PATERNITY
PUZZLE

CHAPTER ONE

SAWYER KEY PUSHED THROUGH THE PRECINCT DOORS WITH the intensity of a Karen who needed to speak to a fast-food restaurant manager. He was hot, hungry, and horny with no immediate relief in sight. His plane should've landed hours ago, giving him plenty of time to shower and visit with Bones and Dolly before presenting himself at the precinct to support the first graduating class of Explorer cadets. Mechanical problems delayed his connecting flight in Chicago, and he'd arrived in Savannah with no time to spare.

He could feel Royce's agitation pulsating in the air like a throbbing heartbeat. His husband classified public speaking as the tenth circle of hell, though he was exceptionally good at it once he got started. It was the anticipation that tipped Royce's natural edginess into irritability. And that's when Sawyer would typically find creative ways to take Royce's mind off the speaking engagement. But they were on the sixth day of a weeklong abstention from sex. They'd shared a very active love life, and to suddenly go without the physical and emotional release had seemed like a huge shock to his system. There wasn't a part of Sawyer's body that didn't ache for Royce's touch, but at least they didn't have to wait much longer.

And the sacrifice would be worth it.

Seeking Royce out before the graduation ceremony under these circumstances was probably a bad idea, but he strode through the corridors with purpose. Something about Sawyer's countenance must've betrayed the surging storm inside him because his colleagues greeted him with a wary nod instead of their usual cheerfulness. He didn't need to follow the drumbeat of Royce's heart to know where to find him; his husband was as predictable as he was sexy. Moments later, Sawyer pushed through the locker room door and took his first easy breath since leaving for the crime convention on Sunday afternoon. Royce stood in front of a sink with his hands braced on the porcelain and his head hanging down. The tense lines of his body matched the tight knot in Sawyer's stomach. Four days had passed without kissing the man who owned his soul.

Royce slowly raised his head and met Sawyer's gaze in the mirror. Mercurial gray eyes lit with joy and relief, and wicked lips curved into a smile. But it wasn't long ago that Royce had resented his very existence, viewing Sawyer as an interloper who'd forced himself into a space he wasn't wanted. But that was then, and now, Sawyer's husband wanted him very much.

Royce's body visibly relaxed, and the knot in Sawyer's stomach eased. Straightening to his full height, Royce heaved a dramatic sigh of relief. He pushed off the sink and strode to Sawyer, wrapping him up in a tight embrace. "It's about fucking time." It was one of Royce's endearing phrases that never failed to make Sawyer smile.

The press of Royce's body against his nearly fried Sawyer's synapses, but he managed a hoarse "Mine." Day six. One more day until their dream of fatherhood would become one step closer to reality. Sawyer turned his head and pressed his lips to the sensitive spot just beneath Royce's ear. A shiver of awareness rippled through his husband, triggering a twin reaction in him. Though it killed him, Sawyer put space between them and cupped Royce's face, stroking his thumb over chiseled cheekbone. "Damn, I've missed you." He raked a hungry gaze over Royce, noting the way his dress uniform showed off the sexy, fit body he knew better than his own. One more day until he could reclaim that perfection for himself. "*All* of you."

Royce moaned and stepped free of Sawyer's touch. "Stop looking at me like that. I'm so horny for you I might go off like a rocket." He cocked his head. "Then you'd be the only one providing a sperm sample tomorrow." Royce reached for his belt like he actually meant to follow through with his threat.

"We both agreed to give a sample so the doctor could pick the specimen that looked best for the procedure," Sawyer reminded him.

"And I expressed my concerns about the kind of legacy that comes with the Locke bloodline," Royce countered. "Remember the time my younger brother tried to kill you?"

"It's hard to forget." Sawyer reached for Royce's hand and tugged him closer. "Holly didn't have reservations about continuing the Locke line with your brother." Harper, their six-month-old baby, was the happiest little guy Sawyer had ever seen, and Jace had taken to fatherhood like a duck to water. "And Dru's boys might be moody teenagers now, but your sister has done an amazing job raising them. Your Uncle Jerry is a wonderful man, and he produced amazing kids." Sawyer puffed out his cheeks and slowly exhaled to buy time because his husband wouldn't like what he had to say next.

Royce cocked his head to the side and narrowed his eyes. "Just don't, okay."

"What?" Sawyer had aimed for an innocent tone and expression, but there was a valid reason the community theater hadn't recruited him to star in one of their productions. He'd barely been able to pull off his roles as inanimate objects in grade school plays, and they didn't have any lines.

"You're about to say something nice about Eddie. Please don't."

Royce's relationship with his dad was tumultuous at best, and for valid reasons. Sometimes things were almost good between them, but then conflict would arise and cause a backslide. Sawyer didn't know the source of their current friction, but Royce deserved to hold grudges if that's what he wanted. His husband was also happiest when things were going well with Eddie, so Sawyer couldn't give up on a full reconciliation between them. This wasn't the moment to advocate for Eddie though. It was Royce's big night, so Sawyer held up his hands. "Okay, I won't."

His easy acquiescence did nothing to appease Royce, who sighed and shook his head. "Just say it."

"You just told me not to."

Royce's eyes became the color of thunderclouds to match his rising frustration. "And now I'm telling you to."

"He's trying."

Royce snorted and stepped back. "Yeah, I've believed that in the past, and it's always come back to bite me in the ass." He took a deep breath and exhaled his frustration before glancing down at his watch. "My cadets have worked hard, and they deserve the best from me tonight. And now that my man is back home where he belongs, I can stop moping and give them my full attention." Royce grabbed Sawyer's ass and yanked him into an embrace. "And I have one more night of blue balls before I can give you the best I have."

Sawyer bit back a grin and quirked a brow. "The sterile cup at the fertility clinic is going to be on the receiving end of all that glory tomorrow."

Royce cringed and released his ass. "Just had to ruin it, didn't you?" His voice was all gravel and no glass as desire turned his irises to a molten gunmetal gray.

Sawyer stuck the tip of his tongue out and swiped it over his bottom lip, suddenly feeling like a dance with the devil was in order. "I'll be thinking of you the whole time I'm in the little room tomorrow, working my fist up and down—"

Royce cut him off with a savage kiss. They were all tongues and teeth, their bodies responding to their chemistry like a match to dry paper. Royce pulled free and stalked a few steps away, keeping his back to Sawyer as he readjusted himself.

Sawyer closed his eyes and cycled through meditative breaths to get his body under control. He heard Royce's approach and felt his body heat, but he kept his eyelids shut. He was halfway into another deep inhale when Royce spoke up.

"Trying to meditate?"

Sawyer cocked one eye open. "Uh-huh."

"You think you can just huff and puff away your desire for me?"

Sawyer shrugged. "Never tried it before."

"Well, you can't," Royce said emphatically.

Sawyer snapped his eye shut again and pulled another long breath into his lungs. *One more day. One more day.* "I am feeling in better control now," he lied.

Royce moved in close enough that his breath ghosted over Sawyer's neck. Sharp teeth nipped his earlobe and tugged. "Tell that to your dick, Asshole. That bastard is hard enough to drive steel." Royce's hand landed on Sawyer's hip. "Or me."

Sawyer's next breath was a shaky exhale that became a whimper when Royce's fingers grazed over his erection. "Dickhead."

"I'd planned to work a half day tomorrow, but I've changed my mind," Royce said. Sawyer opened his eyes and locked onto his husband's ravenous gaze. "My first load might end up in a sterile cup at the fertility clinic, but the second one is going to land all over you. I'm going to pump the one after that inside you. I need to mark my territory again."

Sawyer stroked his forefinger over Royce's tie but stopped before reaching his pants. "We're not as young as we used to be," he pointed out. "We could probably finish our workday after the clinic visit before we're fully recovered for round two." Sawyer arched a brow. "And I think three rounds is extremely ambitious."

Royce gripped Sawyer's chin and jerked him forward for a quick kiss. "Challenge accepted." He released Sawyer and stepped a few feet away. "Tell me about the crime conference so I can get my mind off our dicks."

Sawyer chuckled and ran a hand through his hair. "I can barely remember my name right now."

"It will all come flooding back once you start talking," Royce said. "I bet your presentation on solving cold cases was a big hit with the attendees."

"They seemed to like it. Cold-case investigations are a popular topic."

"Did anyone ask for your autograph?" Royce asked.

"What? No. I'm not Jon Bon Jovi."

"You were probably a rock star to the convention attendees and probably some of the other panelists too," Royce countered. "They would've happily plied you with drinks if you'd gone down to the hotel bar each night instead of hanging out with me on FaceTime."

"I'd rather buddy watch TV with you than hang out with strangers. You're my rockstar."

"God, I'm crazy about you." Royce looked down at his dick and sighed. "Crisis diverted for now."

Sawyer's erection had subsided too, but his balls felt like they weighed five pounds each. They'd only needed to abstain from ejaculating for two to five days before the procedure, but Sawyer's conference stretched that out longer. And his strive for perfection convinced him that abstaining longer increased their odds of success.

A loud, assertive knock made them both look at the door. "Come on, Ro." It was Tara, Royce's fellow Explorer instructor. She'd also married their friend Mel and had become a stepmother to Royce's godchildren. "The cadets are getting restless. Stop making out with your husband, and let's get the show on the road."

"How'd you know Sawyer was in here?"

"He moved through the precinct like a freaking stormtrooper to reach you," Tara said.

Royce's eyes softened when they met Sawyer's. "Aww."

"I told you I missed you."

Royce pressed a quick kiss to Sawyer's lips before striding to the door. He pulled it open and gestured for Sawyer to exit first.

"Thank goodness you're back," Tara said to Sawyer, then hooked a thumb in Royce's direction. "This guy has been a whiny brat since you've been gone."

"Have not." If a voice could pout, Royce's would've stomped its feet too.

Tara just rolled her eyes before leading them down the corridor. "He constantly checked the convention's website and social media accounts, looking for photos and videos of you."

It was Sawyer's turn to get all warm and gooey inside. "Aww."

Royce rolled his eyes. "It was only once or twice while you were away."

"More like once or twice an hour," Tara argued.

Instead of responding to his partner's dig, Royce hummed the music that played whenever the stormtroopers entered a scene in the *Star Wars* movies. Sawyer looped an arm around Royce's shoulders, pulled him closer, and whispered, "I have an idea for our next Halloween costumes. You can be Darth Vader, and I'll be a storm-trooper who drops to his knees and services you on command."

Royce sucked in a sharp breath and nearly stumbled, but he righted himself and blessed Sawyer with a wicked smile. "Welcome to the dark side."

They paused outside the community room doors to go their separate ways. Royce's cadets were waiting for him in the cafeteria so they could file into the room together, and Sawyer needed to find a seat among the family members and supporters in attendance. Sawyer winked at his husband before ducking inside the packed room. It looked like every seat was taken, and he'd resigned himself to standing at the back of the room when a familiar face snagged his attention. Her stunning images had graced magazine covers for five decades, and she used her success and fame to make the world a better place through activism. The world called this paragon of perfection Evangeline O'Neal, one of the first women to put the super in supermodel, but Sawyer called her Mom. She stuck her arm up in the air and waved him over. That's when he noticed the empty chair beside her and the rest of the occupants in the row. Barron Key, his newly retired father, wasn't a surprise, and neither were Jace and Holly. When Sawyer first started working for Savannah PD, he'd resented Holly, thinking she and Royce had something romantic going on. Then Sawyer had discovered they were childhood best friends, and Holly was head over heels in love with a different Locke brother. Now, she investigated cold cases with Sawyer and was the one who'd convinced him to give a presentation at the conference.

When he reached the end of the aisle, Sawyer's gaze locked on the seventy-year-old version of his husband sitting beside Jace. Sawyer wasn't sure if he was more surprised about Eddie's attendance or the effort he'd put into his appearance. He'd only seen Royce's father in T-shirts and faded jeans. Eddie wore a pale blue polo shirt with a pair of dark denim jeans. His hair was more gray than blond now, but it only made him more attractive. Eddie hadn't noticed him yet because he was too busy talking to the infant he cradled in his arms. Harper stared intently at his grandfather's face and appeared to be hanging on to his every word. Sawyer wished Royce was there to witness the interaction.

"I told you he liked me," Eddie said, turning to look at Jace. That's when he noticed Sawyer standing there. A hesitant smile curved the older man's mouth. Eddie liked Sawyer well enough, but he still seemed uncomfortable around him and his family, though Evangeline went out of her way to include him. "You made it."

"Barely," Sawyer said with a smile. "It's good to see you, Eddie. Thanks for coming."

His father-in-law's cheeks turned a little pink, and he nodded before returning his attention to the baby, who'd grabbed his beard with both his chubby hands.

Sawyer greeted everyone as he shuffled along the row until he reached the empty chair. He leaned down and kissed his mother's cheek before sitting beside her. "Thanks for saving a seat for me," he said.

"Of course. How was Denver?"

Before he could answer, Tara and Royce entered the front of the community room, and Sawyer's full attention went straight to his husband. The nerves from earlier had completely disappeared. The man who approached the podium stood tall and proud as he smiled at the audience. Royce's gaze landed on him and lingered for only a few seconds, but it was enough to make Sawyer's pulse race.

Evangeline leaned closer and whispered, "Breathe, darling."

Sawyer chuckled with his exhale. "I'm always in awe that he's my husband." His chest swelled with pride as Royce addressed the room.

"Wow, this is quite a crowd for a Thursday night." He turned to Tara and said, "Sergeant South, we either grossly underestimated the turnout or some of these people wound up here by mistake." He faced forward again. "If you're here to see a concert, you probably meant to go to the Savannah Civic Center." The remark earned a chuckle from the crowd, and when no one got up to leave, Royce said. "Note to self: find a larger venue next year. But seriously, thank you all for coming. It means a lot to Sergeant South and me, and I know the cadets will be thrilled to see how many people showed up to celebrate their achievements. And we probably shouldn't keep them waiting any longer. Please stand and welcome your Explorer cadets."

The kids strode proudly into the room to excited applause. Royce let them soak it in for a few minutes before asking everyone to take their seats. He led the commencement exercises with humor and heart, celebrating two years of the cadets' training that included a video highlight reel of their finest moments. Commissioner Rigby spoke to the cadets about their bright futures, and Chief Mendoza passed out scholarships to some of them. Afterward, the chief remained at the podium to call out the cadets' names so Tara and Royce could pass out the certificates and shake their hands. The ceremony only took an hour, but Sawyer suspected Royce would take just as long to pose for photos with his cadets and their families.

"Harper is getting a little fussy," Holly said. "We're going to head out so we can feed him."

"Tell Royce we'll call him later," Jace added.

"Thanks for coming." Sawyer smacked an exaggerated kiss against Harper's chubby cheek before hugging the baby's parents.

Eddie cooed something at Harper that made the baby smile at him. Eddie hugged Jace and Holly, and Sawyer noticed he held on to his oldest son longer than usual. *He's trying, damn it.* Eddie watched the trio leave before meeting Sawyer's gaze. "I'm probably going to head out too. Not sure Royce wanted me to be here, but it felt like the right thing to do." He cleared his throat and rocked back on his heels. "And I wanted to be here."

"He's always happy to see you, Eddie," Sawyer told him. And it was true, no matter what Royce said. Whenever Eddie showed up, it meant there was a chance for them. "He's probably going to be a while though. Would you like to meet us at Joe's and get a drink?"

Eddie lifted his hand and rubbed the back of his neck. His son had a similar gesture when presented with chores he didn't want to do. Royce would rather remodel a room from the bare studs than do the dishes. "That's the cop bar, right?"

"It's a bar where some cops like to hang out. Joe's isn't exclusive to SPD. They serve amazing chicken wings."

"And jalapeño poppers," Evangeline said as she joined them.

Eddie looked surprised. Was it because Evangeline preferred bar food or that she was familiar with Joe's? "Is the invitation to your family barbecue still good?"

"Of course," Evangeline said, placing her hand on Barron's back. "My husband has become quite the pit master since retiring."

"Oh, I don't know about that," Barron replied. "But I give it my all."

Eddie nodded. "Would you mind if I bring a guest?"

"Of course not. Who's the lucky lady?" Evangeline asked.

Eddie shoved his hands in his front pockets, and he rocked back on his heels again. "A new friend."

"A special friend?" Evangeline asked, waggling her brows.

Barron snorted and shook his head. "You don't have to answer her." But Eddie's shy grin said his friend was definitely special, maybe even VIP. "You can bring whomever you like. The more the merrier."

"Thanks, I appreciate it." Eddie nodded in Sawyer's direction. "Glad you made it home safely. I'll see you guys on Sunday."

"Thanks for coming," Sawyer said.

Eddie held up a hand as he walked away.

"It always surprises me just how much Royce looks like his dad," Evangeline said.

Sawyer watched Eddie walk away, noting Royce even carried himself like his dad. "All his kids favor him in one way or another."

"Strong genes," Evangeline said.

"Very."

Sawyer forced his attention away from Eddie to find his mother studying him closely. He hadn't told Evangeline about their appointment at the fertility clinic, but she possessed a sixth sense where her children were concerned. Had something in Sawyer's voice given him away? Evangeline would be so excited for them if she knew what they had planned. Her brow rose inquisitively, and Sawyer was on the verge of confessing when Commissioner Rigby approached. He used the interruption to make a break for it and was relieved when Chief Mendoza struck up a conversation with him about the convention. His father caught his attention a few minutes later, gesturing that they were heading out. Sawyer waved goodbye and breathed easier. He continued to make small talk until Royce finished taking photos.

"I'm ready to get out of this uniform," Royce said when he joined Sawyer. "Did you still want to go to Joe's, or…"

Sawyer followed him out of the community center and back toward the locker room. *Or* meant going home alone, where they couldn't have sex. It was better to kill a few hours in public where they'd have to keep their hands to themselves.

"My mom got me in the mood for wings and jalapeño poppers now," Sawyer said.

"You don't like junk food."

"It's the only vice I can indulge in tonight," Sawyer pointed out. "I can't drink a beer. I can't have you. There's no way I'm going to eat a damn salad with grilled chicken on it."

Royce chuckled and patted him on the back. "Do you think anyone will notice if neither of us has a beer?"

"Maybe, but we'll come up with an excuse if someone mentions it," Sawyer said.

"I saw your parents in the audience. They're so thoughtful."

"They weren't the only parental support you had tonight," Sawyer said.

Royce nudged him with his elbow. "Stop gloating. I'll text Eddie and thank him for coming."

"Or you can tell him in person on Sunday when he comes to the cookout at my parents' house."

Royce stopped suddenly. "Eddie is coming to their Memorial Day party?"

"Yep."

"Evangeline has invited him to every occasion at her house, but he's never attended before. Why now?"

Sawyer rolled his eyes. "Stop being so suspicious. He's not casing the joint to rob my parents blind. I keep telling you. He's—"

"Trying. I know." Royce continued down the hallway, and Sawyer naturally followed him. Stopping at the locker room door, Royce turned to face him. "You can't come in here with me."

"Because you're mad at me about Eddie?"

"Because I'm mad with lust," Royce countered. "Six. Damn. Days."

Longing knotted Sawyer's guts. "It's been torture."

Royce rested his hand on Sawyer's hip and squeezed. "I'll only be a few minutes."

"Be back in five minutes, or I'll come looking for you."

"Don't threaten me with a good time," Royce said with a wink before disappearing into the locker room. He had thirty seconds to spare when he returned with a duffle bag slung over his shoulder and a cocky grin on his face. "Let's enjoy some wings and darts."

"And jalapeño poppers."

The usual suspects were at Joe's, helping to distract Sawyer from the lust clawing at his guts. He assuaged some of his hunger with tasty bar food he'd probably regret later. No one asked why they weren't drinking or commented on their early departure. Sawyer would take his wins where he could get them. They drove home in separate vehicles since Sawyer had come straight from the airport. Royce snagged his suitcase from the trunk and rolled it into the laundry room. Sawyer was usually the one who insisted on throwing the clothes in the washing machine as soon as he walked through the door, but he figured Royce was just trying to stay busy.

"Where are my babies?" Sawyer said when he entered the living room.

Dolly, the Yorkie that had adopted them, jumped off the couch and hurled herself at Sawyer. She released a series of high-pitched barks until he squatted down and picked her up. FaceTime chats with Royce had included the pets, so he'd seen the adorable Americana-themed hair ribbon the groomer had used to keep Dolly's long bangs out of her eyes. It looked even cuter in person though.

"Evangeline is going to eat you up on Monday."

She called Dolly and Bones her grandpup and grandkitty and spoiled them rotten, but Sawyer knew she was eager for them to have a baby. And just where was the king of the house? Sawyer called Bones' name, and the massive gray Maine coon cat strolled out of the hallway.

"There's my best boy." Sawyer set Dolly on the ground and picked up Bones. Maybe it was the drastic change between the tiny dog and massive cat, but it felt like Bones had gained weight in his absence. "How many treats have you gone through since Saturday?" Bones responded with a head butt to the chin and a loud purring that rumbled his massive body.

"He missed you," Royce said. "We all did."

Sawyer turned and found Royce watching him with a fond smile on his face. "I missed you guys too." He set Bones down and moved toward Royce but stopped when his husband held up a hand.

"I think we should probably sleep in different beds. I don't trust myself."

Sawyer wanted to protest, but Royce looked like he was barely hanging on to his control. "Okay." He sounded as miserable as Royce looked. "Just one more night."

Royce closed the gap between them and kissed Sawyer's lips. "Then I'm taking you to bed, and we're going to stay there until the pool party on Saturday night."

CHAPTER TWO

A WHIRRING HUM PENETRATED ROYCE'S SLEEP, AND HE groaned his irritation into the lumpy pillow. Discomfort had kept him awake until two o'clock in the morning, and the rude awakening triggered his brain to play a game called "What hurts the most?" Was it his back from this crappy mattress, his neck from the shitty pillow, or his aching balls from lack of sex? A hot shower could cure two of his ailments, but it would make it harder to ignore the third. Clearly, Sawyer was in an anxious state if he'd dragged the vacuum out already. The machine switched off, and Royce breathed a sigh of relief. Maybe he could sleep a little longer before he had to get ready for their appointment at the fertility clinic.

"Oh, yeah. That's the spot."

Sawyer's husky morning voice reached him through the wall separating the bedrooms, and he forgot all about his aching back and neck. Blood rushed to his dick as he imagined eliciting those same words from his husband lips. Sawyer's body would be warm from sleep as Royce kissed a path down his stomach. Strong thighs would part to make room for him and—

"Mmmmm. Yeah, get in there, James," Sawyer urged.

"Wait a fucking minute." Royce threw back the covers, stormed to their bedroom, and shoved the door open so hard it crashed against the wall. "Who the hell is James?"

Sawyer was sitting up in bed, propped up against the headboard with a mound of perfect pillows to support his lower back. A smug smile graced his face before he lifted a steaming mug of herbal tea to his lips and took a sip. Caffeine was on the no-no list, and they'd gone longer without that than sex. His husband had adjusted well with a variety of caffeine-free options, while Royce had relied on hot water with lemon slices. Sawyer looked so damn delicious that Royce forgot why he'd charged into their bedroom like it was a SWAT mission.

"Good morning." Sawyer's voice was a silky purr that begged Royce to join him between the sheets. "Did you sleep well?"

"Huh?" Royce shook his head to clear the lust fog muddling his thoughts "No, I fucking did not. Do we hate our friends and family?"

Sawyer arched a brow. "Pardon me?"

"That mattress is as hard as a rock, and those pillows provide no support." Royce placed his hands on his lower back and arched his spine before flexing his neck from side to side. "We need to upgrade the guest room before the baby comes. People will want to help us for the first few weeks, and the least we can do is provide a comfortable place for them to rest."

"You mean my mom will want to move in," Sawyer said.

The whirring sound fired back up again before Royce could respond. A wet, brushing sound joined the symphony of noises. He spun around to the television and watched as a carpet-cleaning machine moved over a soapy round rug. A camera panned back to give a broader view of the action, and that's when Royce noticed the googly eyes affixed to the carpet cleaner. The black pupils bounced and shifted as the machine moved across the screen. The sounds and motions were nearly hypnotic, and Royce's breathing evened out as he watched. Then he noticed the name of the machine painted in a script. He turned to face his husband with a quirked brow. "Dirt Reynolds?"

Sawyer grinned from ear to ear. "Isn't he cute? Sometimes James puts a cowboy hat on him."

"It's creative, for sure." Royce looked at the TV again. "I assume James is the person wearing the white rubber boots and pushing Dirt Reynolds around."

"Yep."

"Is this a new kink?" Royce asked.

Sawyer laughed, bringing Royce's full attention to his husband's naked torso. "The hum of the machine and the back-and-forth action is relaxing. I'm not the only one who thinks so. This video has millions of views."

There was no denying the video's effect on Sawyer. His guy was a go-getter. He didn't lounge in bed and drink hot beverages unless they were on vacation, and Sawyer only sounded this relaxed after sex. They were kicking off a four-day weekend, so that might've contributed to the lounging, but it didn't explain why Sawyer sounded so chill. His husband wouldn't have taken so much as an herbal supplement to reduce his innate restlessness with his sperm donation looming. And then the source of Sawyer's contentedness became crystal clear. "We're making a baby today," Royce said.

Sawyer's answering smile was the most beautiful thing Royce had ever seen. "Yes, we are."

Up to this point, they'd used different terms to describe the process. They were going to try for a baby. They were hoping to have a baby. Royce's inner dialogue had included the same gentle optimism, and he was sure Sawyer was just as cautious. Try. Hope. But something had shifted overnight, and cautiousness had given way to certainty.

Whatever hesitance he'd harbored over donating a sample had also evaporated. Royce would do anything to keep that smile on his husband's face, though he still hoped Sawyer's sperm would come out the victor.

"As long as you put some clothes on or leave the room," Sawyer said. "Damn, you are one sexy man."

Royce squelched the urge to flex and preen as he crossed the room to their dresser. He yanked out a pair of lounge pants from a drawer and pulled them on. Then he climbed onto the bed and accepted the mug Sawyer extended to him. Just that slight brush of fingers was enough to stir trouble below his waistband, but Royce could tamp it down one more time for a wonderful cause. He sipped the brown liquid and recognized it as chamomile. His Aunt Tipsy had sworn it cured anything, but she'd never convinced Royce. He got distracted by the action on the television and ended up taking another sip out of habit. Still not coffee and still not a fan. "When did your rug-cleaning fetish start?"

"I discovered this YouTube channel when I was trying to kill time at the conference. And it's not a fetish," Sawyer protested.

"That's the spot. Oh yeah. Get in there, James." Royce might've injected too much breathiness into his imitation because Sawyer bit his bottom lip and squirmed.

"I didn't say any of that," he protested.

"You did. Word for word."

Sawyer snatched the mug back hard enough to make the liquid slosh over the side. He scowled at Royce like the brown spot on the duvet was his fault. "And I sure as hell didn't sound like Marilyn Monroe when she serenaded JFK for his birthday."

"I might've embellished, but only slightly."

The sounds on the television shifted to running water, and Royce turned to see what was happening next. A new camera angle showed a masculine hand spraying the rug with a thick hose. Royce was going to comment on the suggestive nature of the imagery, but the view changed to the water running out of the rug. The screen went black, and Royce scowled at Sawyer, who looked smug as hell with the remote in his hand. Give a guy some power, and look out.

"Hey! You turned it off during the money shot," Royce complained.

"Do you want to lounge in bed all day or eat breakfast and go make our baby?"

Royce perked up. "Real bacon or the fake stuff?" Sawyer's commitment to healthier food options was admirable most of the time, but not when it came to breakfast meats. He'd tried to lure Royce over to the dark side, aka turkey bacon or chicken sausage, but Royce had remained faithful to pork.

"The real stuff." Sawyer winked. "You'll need the protein boost, and you deserve a special reward."

Royce probably should've protested the bit where Sawyer treated him like a dog who performed a trick or a cat who remembered to bury his poop in the litter box. But the promise of real bacon kept his yap shut.

"I've got bacon duties, and you can make the eggs," Royce said.

"Scrambled or fried?"

They'd had similar conversations many times over the past five years, an easy back-and-forth about food prep and who would do what. They were ordinary tasks, yet the morning felt extraordinary because their lives were about to change. There'd be a third person to consider when making the simplest decisions. A tiny person with big needs who'd rely on them for everything. Royce waited for panic to surge or doubt to surface, but a sense of calm washed over him, and confidence stiffened his resolve.

He reached for Sawyer's hand and laced their fingers together. "Let's go with scrambled."

Sawyer's lips parted, but no sound escaped. He cleared his throat and tried again. His voice was thick with emotion when he said, "Thank you."

"For choosing scrambled?" Royce teased.

Sawyer's brown eyes softened to melted chocolate. "For everything."

Royce leaned in for a quick kiss and got out of there before he tackled his husband to the bed. He showered in the guest bathroom, where he kept the water cold and his hands moving. Lingering in specific places for too long was tempting fate. "Not long now, buddy." Consoling his dick in a buck-up-little-camper voice was sinking to a new low, but at least no one was around to witness his shame.

"I heard that," Sawyer said from the other side of the door.

"You can talk to him later." When Sawyer didn't answer, Royce rinsed himself and turned off the shower. "Preferably on your knees," he murmured. Royce reached around the shower curtain to grab his towel off the rack, but his hand only found air. "What the hell?"

"Looking for this?" Sawyer's teasing tone had Royce whisking the shower curtain back with more force than necessary. His husband held the fluffy towel in his hand and lifted it like a trophy. Challenge sparked in his dark eyes, daring Royce to come and get it. And oh, how he wanted to, but two could play this game.

Propping his elbow against the shower wall, Royce smirked at Sawyer. "You should've just said so if you wanted to see me naked. There was no need to sneak in here all ninja-like."

Sawyer raked his teeth over his bottom lip as his gaze devoured Royce's wet, naked body. Dark, hungry eyes snapped up to meet his. A brow arched high, and Sawyer's expression turned haughty. "Did you say you wanted me to talk to your dick?"

"Yeah, I did," Royce said. "From your knees."

Sawyer's nostrils flared, and his chest expanded with a deep inhale. "We'll be lucky to limp away from this weekend."

"Yeah, but we'll make it hurt so good," Royce told him.

"I gotta get out of here." Sawyer abruptly turned and left the bathroom. "Thirty minutes."

"Hey! Can I have my towel?"

Sawyer reappeared in the doorframe and lobbed it at him. Royce snatched it out of the air but didn't cover his body. Sawyer took one last look at Royce before emitting a low growl and ducking out of the room. Royce rubbed the towel over his head to wick away the excess water and then moved lower. What did a guy wear to a fertility clinic to donate sperm for a future child? He wanted to present himself as a suitable candidate for fatherhood, but what did that look like? Eddie wore faded jeans, Harley Davidson shirts, and sometimes a leather vest. Barron Key's idea of casual wear included khaki pants and a pressed polo shirt.

"Twenty-five minutes, Dickhead!" Sawyer called down the hallway. "I'm starting the bacon, and I don't want to hear any complaints that it's too chewy or too crispy."

"You better watch your choice of endearments during our appointment, Asshole," Royce returned. "They won't give us a baby."

"They have no say in the matter. They're not an adoption agency. We're paying them to transfer our viable sperm inside Kelsey's uterus."

Transferring sounded way more clinical than blasting it in there with a syringe and a tube. "We can't afford to take chances," Royce said. "That's why I can't figure out what to wear." He'd put on something similar to Sawyer, but the heat in his husband's eyes had distracted him from noticing the clothes he'd chosen. "What are you wearing?"

"You just saw me."

"We're probably down to twenty-three minutes," Royce pointed out. "And you know damn well why I didn't notice your clothes."

"Jeans, a plain blue T-shirt, and tennis shoes."

Royce shrugged and grabbed a gray shirt, jeans, and underwear from his drawers and dressed hastily. When he reached the kitchen, Sawyer had breakfast going on the stove. Royce stepped up behind him and wrapped his arms around Sawyer's waist. The bacon grease popped in the skillet, and some of it splattered on his arm. He opened the cabinet next to the stove, removed a grease splatter screen, and set it on top of the skillet.

"Can't believe I forgot that nifty tool," Sawyer said. "I'm the one who showed you how to use it."

"You're just really excited about today and probably running on autopilot." Royce looked around the room. "Where are the fur children?"

"Off pouting somewhere." Sawyer stepped aside so Royce could take over the bacon duties while he started on the eggs. "I got stingy with their treats this morning when I noticed how much lighter the bags had gotten in my absence."

Busted. "But we missed you so much."

Sawyer's mouth curved into a wry smile. "That's what I took Bones' and Dolly's pitiful meows and yips to mean."

"Did it work?"

A dark brow shot upward. "What do you think?"

"I think they're hiding somewhere and crying," Royce teased.

"And how did you compensate for your loneliness?"

Royce pursed his lips together so he wouldn't confess to the number of bear claws he'd eaten while Sawyer was in Denver.

"You had a pastry palooza, didn't you?" Sawyer pressed. "A gluten gluttony."

"We only have fifteen minutes before we need to leave to make our baby." Royce's deflection was a cheap trick, but a very useful one because Sawyer's face lit up like a Christmas tree.

"Want to hear about the dream I had last night?" Sawyer asked.

Royce growled and waggled his brows. "Was I there?"

Sawyer leaned in for a quick kiss. "Always." A wistful expression softened his features. "I dreamed we had a little girl." He turned and looked at Royce. "And she was a little spitfire, just like you."

A boulder formed in Royce's throat. "I would love to have a daughter with you." Staring into Sawyer's eyes would cause a burned breakfast and give them a late start to the clinic, so he kept his attention on finishing the bacon. "What did we name her?"

"I didn't get that far," Sawyer said. "Maybe one of us said it, but I got swept away by our daughter's perfection." He finished the eggs and moved the skillet to the back burner. "Do you want toast, or do you plan on making a breakfast burrito?"

"Burrito," Royce said as he transferred their perfectly cooked bacon to a plate lined with paper towels.

Sawyer rummaged around in the refrigerator to find the condiments Royce preferred on his burrito. He set the hot sauce, Duke's mayonnaise, shredded cheese, and sliced jalapeños on the counter. "Your sperm are going to think they're little Don Juans today."

Royce cupped Sawyer's neck and dragged him closer. "And yours are going to think they're Ted Mullins, always following the rules and paying their credit card bills early." Sawyer shook with laughter until Royce kissed him hard. "I can't wait for our Dons and Teds to play together when we get back home." Sawyer's breath sounded shaky, and his pulse hammered in his throat. "We're probably down to twelve minutes now."

"Ten," Sawyer said as he stared at Royce's mouth. "One more."

Royce gave in but was careful to keep a gap between their bodies. He released Sawyer and stepped back. "Time to power up."

Sawyer laughed and shook his head. "You sound like a cartoon character about to go into battle."

"It's going to be survival of the fittest today," Royce said as he assembled a burrito. "Only the strong can swim upstream and charm the lady eggs, so it's more like an episode of *Gladiators*."

Sawyer scrubbed a hand over his face. "Please don't narrate the procedure today."

"Sperm, ready? 'You will go on my first whistle.'" Royce's imitation of the show's host made Sawyer groan. "I had to get it out of my system, and I'll be on my best behavior now."

"Famous last words."

They arrived at the clinic fifteen minutes before their appointment, which in Sawyer's universe meant they were late. Royce was raised by a selfish man who'd thought the party wouldn't start until he arrived. Sawyer tried to play it cool, but Royce saw the vein pulsing at his temple.

"I don't think Kelsey is here yet," Sawyer said.

"She'll be here. I would imagine mornings frequently go sideways with Ella." Royce knew their amazing friend was just as excited about the process as they were. She was the one who'd volunteered to be their egg donor and surrogate on their wedding day, and she'd never wavered from her commitment. Before Royce could remind Sawyer of that, Kelsey pulled up beside them and parked her car.

Sawyer turned to look at Royce, his eyes wide with excitement and awe. "I'm not dreaming, right? This is really happening."

Royce took off his seat belt and leaned across the console to kiss him. "Hell yeah, it is." He pushed the release button on Sawyer's seat belt too. "Let's not keep your best girl waiting."

They got out of their SUV and greeted Kelsey with warm hugs. Unlike them, the former fashion model turned cybercrime fighter had dressed for the special occasion in a knee-length floral ivory dress. Espadrille sandals turned her into a six-foot-tall goddess and showed off her mile-long legs. Kelsey's dark brown skin shimmered beneath the sun, and she smelled like jasmine and vanilla. She'd piled her hair on top of her head so that the black coils cascaded around to frame her face.

"You always look beautiful, but today, you're glowing," Royce said.

"Hydration and moisturizer." Kelsey pushed her sunglasses on top of her head and winked. "And Black don't crack. You guys ready to do this?"

Royce and Sawyer locked eyes and smiled.

Kelsey giggled. "Yeah, you are."

The clinic's waiting room was more upscale than those in most physicians' offices. It had comfortable couches, love seats, and club chairs in cheerful pastel colors instead of the dull modular-style chairs Royce was used to seeing. They'd painted the walls a cool, pale gray and placed clusters of lush potted plants throughout the room. There were several magazines on top of the coffee table in front of the couch they'd chosen. Most were of the home and lifestyle variety, but some offered the latest celebrity gossip, and there was a medicine journal that caught Royce's eye. A handsome, gray-haired man with icy blue eyes and a cocky smirk stared up at him. The caption beneath the photo read: Jean Claude Matisse, a trailblazer in fertility medicine.

Royce wasn't in the mood to read about celebrities, find a new recipe, or get more gardening ideas. He wouldn't understand a word written in the medical magazine, so he looked for a different distraction. A large aquarium with colorful fish took up a large portion of the opposite wall, and following a betta fish's feisty antics settled Royce's nerves. Beside him, Sawyer anxiously drummed his thumbs against his knees. Royce reached over and took Sawyer's hand. Tense fingers relaxed as they slid between his, and Royce gave them an assuring squeeze.

"Watch the fish. They'll calm you down." Royce figured most patients were anxious about their visits, and he didn't think the fish were there for purely aesthetic reasons.

"Doubtful," Sawyer whispered. He stretched his neck to the left and right, cycled through a deep breath, and gave his full attention to the aquarium. After only a minute or two, Sawyer's breathing returned to normal, and the tension in his shoulders eased. "It's working. You're going to want a fancy tank now, and I know nothing about keeping fish alive."

Royce nudged him with his elbow and tried to keep the smile from his voice when he said, "I hadn't thought about it until you mentioned it."

"Crap," Sawyer mumbled.

"Just kidding. I'm not looking to add to the menagerie."

A door to the right of the waiting room opened, and a twenty-something guy with auburn hair and light eyes stood in the doorway. "Kelsey," he called out.

Royce's mind went blank. They'd gone over the procedure in fine detail during their last visit, but he couldn't remember a single step. His heart pumped frantically, and blood rushed through his veins at an alarming rate. Were they supposed to go with her, or would they get called back separately? The answer was somewhere inside his paralyzed brain.

"Hey." Sawyer's calm voice penetrated his panic.

Royce blinked and looked at his husband. There was a question in his warm, dark eyes. Sawyer wanted to know if Royce was sure about this. Yes. A thousand percent yes. He nodded, and they stood together to follow Kelsey. The ginger-haired physician's assistant introduced himself as Greg. Then he handed Royce and Sawyer sterilized sperm collection cups that were labeled with their names and had barcodes on them. Greg directed them to the private rooms and instructed them to turn in the samples to the lab at the end of the hallway once they finished.

"Are you going to attend the procedure with Kelsey?" Greg asked.

"Yes," Royce and Sawyer said together.

They wouldn't stand down by the business end of the exam table during the procedure, but they would be with Kelsey every step of the way.

"She'll be in suite five." Greg gestured in the opposite direction. "End of the hallway on the right."

"Thanks." Royce placed his hand on the center of Sawyer's back and guided him toward the row of private donation rooms. When Sawyer stopped at the first open door, Royce halted, too, instead of continuing past.

"What are—"

Royce nudged Sawyer into a room the size of a coat closet and followed him inside. He shut the door and locked it before crowding his husband against the opposite wall. Sawyer's mouth curved into a wicked smile, and Royce just had to taste it. He moved in fast but kept the pressure light, more of a tease than anything. He ran the back of his fingers over the front of Sawyer's pants, tracing the outline of his dick and chuckling softly when it responded.

"This is so inappropriate," Sawyer whispered against his lips. "But I'll never forgive you if you stop." He reached between them and stroked Royce too.

A week had passed since he'd felt Sawyer's touch. Blood rushed south almost as fast as it had when he was a horny teenager. It had probably been just as long since over-the-clothes groping had revved him up so much. "It's been so long, and this feels so good." Royce kissed a path down Sawyer's neck and then back up to his ear. "Get your dick out and jerk off into that cup. I want to watch."

"Fuck," Sawyer whimpered as he fumbled with his belt. "How can you make this so sexy?"

"It's a gift," Royce quipped.

Sawyer shoved his pants and underwear down to his upper thighs, and his erection sprang free. Royce moved to the side where he could observe without getting in the way. He double-checked the name on the cup before breaking the seal. Royce gave it to Sawyer, who held it nearby when he took his dick in hand.

"I love your cock even more than my own," Royce growled huskily. He placed his hand on the small of Sawyer's back and slid it down to where the tips of his fingers brushed the upper swells of his bare ass. "I can't wait to feel it buried inside me tonight." Royce kissed the side of Sawyer's neck, watching him stroke faster until his jaw tensed and his motions became jerkier. He was so close. "I love you."

Sawyer gritted his teeth and released into the cup without making a noise. Royce secured the lid and set the container on the little ledge on the opposite side of the wall. Sawyer didn't bother pulling his pants back up when he turned his full attention to Royce. "You're going to pay for this."

"Why am I in trouble? I just wanted to make this less awkward for us."

Sawyer assumed the assertive role and placed his hand on the center of Royce's chest. He bunched his shirt and slowly dragged it upward until it exposed his abdomen and pecs. Sawyer brushed his thumb over Royce's hardened nipple and smiled at the sharp intake of air. "Better get those pants down before it's too late."

Royce happily complied, biting his lips to keep from embarrassing himself, and took his cock in hand. His head fell back against the wall, and Royce started to close his eyes until he remembered that his aim counted this time. Sawyer readied the cup, then lowered his head to suck an extended nipple into his mouth.

"Fuck me," Royce growled.

Sawyer put his mouth to Royce's ear. "Planning to." He dropped his hand and squeezed Royce's ass. "Going to ride this so damn hard tonight."

Royce's entire body tensed as pleasure detonated inside him. He moved the cup in place just in time to collect his sample. Sawyer smiled and kissed him as he came down from his high, panting like he'd just completed a marathon. "My legs haven't felt this shaky since you talked me into riding that massive roller coaster at Cedar Point last summer."

Sawyer chuckled and took the sperm collection from his shaking hands. He screwed the lid on and set it on the ledge next to his sample. Sawyer kissed Royce and tugged his pants into place. "Will you be able to walk to suite five?"

"Do you think they'll mind if I stretch out on one of the couches in the waiting room first?"

"Probably so." Sawyer finished putting Royce back together and kissed him again. "We'll go home and lounge around the pool. We can have a private season opening before our friends come over tomorrow night."

"Mmmm. Sounds nice." A noise outside the room snapped Royce back to reality, and he knew they needed to get going before someone came looking for them. "Feeling sturdier now."

"Good." When Royce reached for the doorknob, Sawyer stopped him. "I love you too."

Most people in their shoes would probably ease the door open, peek outside, and try to hide their naughty behavior. Not him. Royce opened the door and stepped out into the corridor without a care in the world.

Sawyer had his feet firmly planted in the former group. "Is the coast clear?"

"Yep."

Royce felt downright giddy as they casually strolled to the lab drop-off window, where the technicians didn't meet their eyes when they accepted the sample. Had they made too much noise and alerted the entire office to their activities?

"Do you think they know what we did?" Sawyer whispered when they walked away.

"Considering where we are and what our roles are, I'm pretty sure they know what we did."

Sawyer huffed in frustration. "Of course they know we jacked off into a cup, but do you think they know we did it together?"

His mortification was darling. Royce turned his head and quirked a brow. "Do you really care if they did?"

Sawyer chuckled and shook his head. "I should, but I don't."

"And with any luck, we won't need to make a repeat trip to the lab."

Royce knocked on the door to suite five, and Kelsey called out for them to come in. Sawyer entered the room first, and Royce followed him inside. The examination table was inclined at one end, and Kelsey reclined against it, looking like a regal queen even in a disposable gown with a paper blanket covering her lower half. Royce already knew from a previous visit that stirrups came out of the business end of the table. Kelsey looked from one of them to the other before a wide grin spread across her face. Royce could tell that she wanted to razz them about their newly relaxed state.

"Go ahead," he said. "You deserve to give us shit after all the blood tests, ultrasounds, and ovulation tracking you've had to do." In comparison, their week of abstaining was minor.

Kelsey covered her mouth and gave in to the giggles. "It's like a night-and-day difference. You were wound so tight before your trip to the little rooms that the slightest wind would've broken you. And now you look like you've shared a joint."

Sawyer snorted and shook his head while Royce held up his forefinger and mouthed, "One room."

She giggled harder, and Sawyer's face turned bright red as he stared incredulously at Royce.

"That was a tiny down payment for the things she's going to endure over the next nine months." Royce turned to Kelsey. "Anything else you want to know?"

"So many things, but I might not be able to look either of you in the eyes if you tell me," Kelsey said. As if she and Sawyer didn't gossip about him and Andrew on a regular basis. Royce was probably the one who should be shy about making eye contact. "You're feeling confident the intrauterine insemination will take today, huh?"

Dr. Flores had previously said their probability of success was higher than most based on all the test results, but it wasn't a certainty. Royce looked at Sawyer, who smiled happily. "We are," he said.

Kelsey extended both hands to them. Royce took the right side of her bed, and Sawyer took the left. "I felt the same way when I woke up this morning. This sense of calmness washed over me, and peace filled my heart. I am so honored to be part of this journey. I love you both."

Royce's eyes stung, and he shook his head. "No crying. Not yet."

They were still laughing and holding hands when Dr. Flores

knocked on the door and stepped inside a few minutes later. She greeted them with a warm smile. "Are we ready to do this?"

"We are," the trio said together.

"The sperm samples are nearly identical in concentration, motility, and morphology," Dr. Flores said. "I can't recommend one donor over the other, so this decision comes down to personal choice. Do you know which sample you want my lab to prepare?"

Royce and Sawyer stared into one another's eyes for what seemed like hours. They'd had this debate many times once they decided to do the insemination process, but they could never agree on who would be the biological father. Royce wanted one thing, and Sawyer wanted another. But suddenly, the answer was just there.

"We do," Royce and Sawyer said together.

CHAPTER THREE

SAWYER SMILED AS HE WATCHED THE POOLSIDE SHENANIGANS through his kitchen window. This time next year, their baby would celebrate his or her first Memorial Day weekend. He still felt like they were meant to be dads to the sweetest little girl to ever live. A warm hand settled at the small of his back, and he nearly dropped the tomato he'd just washed. Sawyer would know that touch anywhere and turned to look at his husband, who wore a matching grin.

"I'm worried our mouths are going to stick in this current position," Sawyer said. They hadn't stopped grinning all over themselves since leaving the clinic with Kelsey the previous day. "Your future cadets won't be able to take you seriously."

Royce arched a brow. "And the suspects you interrogate will?"

Conceding the point with a slight nod, Sawyer said, "What are we going to do about it?"

Royce took the tomato from his hand and gently set it on the counter. He cupped Sawyer's face and moved in until their lips nearly touched. "I have an idea." He waggled his brows for emphasis.

Sawyer's blood migrated south as memories of their passionate lovemaking replayed in his mind. Their interlude at the clinic had taken the edge off so that they could act like respectable humans. They'd treated Kelsey to lunch at the Hummingbird Café after the procedure, and then she took them to a mega store that sold anything and everything a parent could want for a new baby. It was overwhelming to say the least, and Sawyer had expected Royce's eyes to glass over like they did every time they went into a store that didn't sell tools or equipment. It turned out that Sawyer had underestimated his husband, but only because there were tons of high-tech gadgetry available for babies and their parents. Royce had wanted to start a registry there and then, and the only way Sawyer could get him out of the store was to whisper some of the wicked things he wanted to do to Royce's body when they got home. They'd barely kept their hands off each other since.

Royce's next words proved he was still trying to make up for lost time. "I just need everyone to go home so I can have you to myself."

They had plans with family over the holiday weekend, but they'd set aside Saturday night for hosting a pool party for their closest friends, who were also their SPD colleagues. Kelsey was the only one from their core squad who had prior commitments she couldn't shake.

Sawyer suppressed a shiver and the urge to drag his husband to their bedroom. "They just got here," he protested. "And shouldn't you be getting the grill ready?"

"I did," Royce replied. "I came in to get the meat and caught you daydreaming."

"Was not."

"Were too. You've stood in the same place for at least two minutes with the tomato suspended in the air. Bet you were thinking about how different our party will look next year."

"Yeah," Sawyer admitted dreamily. "I know it's not smart to get our hopes up so high, but I can't help myself."

"I can't either," Royce admitted. "I did what I promised not to do today."

Sawyer laughed because he knew what Royce was about to divulge. "I texted Kels too," he confessed. "The doctor made me nervous with all the talk about cramping and spotting."

"But she's doing good. No issues so far." Royce pressed a kiss to his neck. "Do you feel different?"

Sawyer smiled again. "Yeah. I feel...giddy. Is that the right word?"

Nodding, Royce said, "Yeah, I don't know how else to describe it. Do I look different?"

Sawyer narrowed his eyes and studied the handsome face he adored so much. "Yeah. You look like you're at ease with your place in the world. Serenity is very attractive on you."

Royce chuckled. "No one would ever describe me as serene. I might be more laid-back than you are, but I have a restless energy that never seems to fade. It feels more like a contented hum right now though. And I like it." He kissed Sawyer gently before pulling back to study him. "And you're glowing like you just spent a day at the spa with your mom and sister."

"Do you think anyone suspects what's going on?"

"I doubt it with this crew," Royce said. "We didn't tell anyone about our plans, and most people will have too much going on in their lives to notice. If they guess, it won't be the end of the world."

"True. But I want to exist in this happy little bubble with you for as long as I can."

They kissed again, lingering until childish giggles dragged Sawyer's attention away from his husband. Jackson Blue stood just inside the open patio door, holding a girl and boy in each of his massive arms. The detective's linebacker size hid a teddy bear's heart, and no one delivered a quicker smile or joke than Blue. His current grin showed off a lot of teeth, and his dark eyes sparkled with humor. He wore swimming trunks and a pair of flip-flops, showing off gleaming dark skin and a mountain of muscle. Blue and his husband had adopted the twins a year ago, and they'd taken to parenting like ducks to water. DeMarcus wore a pair of trunks that matched Blue's, and Zoya wore a pink bathing suit that matched the beads in her braids. Both kids wore inflatable floaties on the arms they'd wrapped around Blue's neck.

Zeke closed the sliding glass door behind them and shook his head when he clocked his husband's mischievous expression. He was shorter and leaner than Blue, but his firefighter's build was impressive as hell. He placed his hand between Blue's shoulder blades and gave him a little nudge. "We have two toddlers we're trying to potty train, Blue." He patted his husband's back. "You can harass your friends later."

The big man nodded his bald head. "And I will."

"Pee pee," Zoya announced.

"Pee pee," DeMarcus mimicked.

"You know the way to the bathroom," Royce said. They'd hosted countless poker nights and gatherings over the years, and their friends were as familiar with their home as Sawyer and Royce were, and that's the way they wanted it. "I'm going to get the burgers and brats going on the grill." He picked the tomato up off the counter and placed it back in Sawyer's hand. "Try not to slice off a finger while daydreaming."

Sawyer wanted to scoff but couldn't with his history. He'd lost track of the number of times he'd embarrassed himself by getting too absorbed in audiobooks and podcasts while performing tasks. It was due more to luck than skill that he'd never hurt himself or others. "Got it. No daydreaming with sharp objects in my hand."

Royce kissed him once more before retrieving the seasoned meats from the refrigerator and going outside. Sawyer set the tomato on the cutting board and returned to the sink to wash the rest of the vegetables he'd need for his topping bar. He had a reputation for being bougie about food, and he would not disappoint. Sawyer made the mango chutney, tomato jam, and the spicy remoulade a few days ago. All he needed to do was cut and arrange the vegetables. He'd worked his way through the tomatoes and lettuce by the time Blue, Zeke, and the kids passed back through.

"How'd it go?" Sawyer asked.

"We made it." Zeke looked at his husband. "But it was close."

Zoya spotted the strawberries on the fruit plate. "Berry!"

"You can have them with dinner, baby girl," Blue said.

"My little princess can have one now," Sawyer told him. "Do you want a berry too, Dee?" The little boy nodded excitedly and clapped. "We never say no to fruit in this house," Sawyer said as he picked the two best berries off the plate for them. Zoya blew him a kiss on their way out the door, and he settled back on his tasks.

Holly came through a few minutes later with a sleeping Harper. His chubby pink cheeks and pale blond hair made him look like a cherub. "I'm just going to put him in his pack-n-play. Want me to wash up and help?"

"Sure." Conversation would help prevent his mind from wandering too far.

Holly joined him a few minutes later, and he assigned her the avocados. "Slices or chunks?" she asked.

"Slices." Sawyer pulled out a second cutting board from the drawer, then handed her a knife, a spoon, and a lemon to squeeze over the fruit to keep it from browning.

"Did you get to enjoy any of the conference presentations between your own speaking engagements?" Holly asked.

"I did," Sawyer replied and listed some of the favorite lectures he attended. "Alec Bishop was there."

Holly set her knife down and looked at him with wide eyes. "Alec Bishop, son of serial killer Andrew Bishop?"

Sawyer chuckled at her expression. "That's the one, and lots of people had that same reaction. They'd kept his involvement a secret until they revealed some surprise panelists and keynote speakers during the kickoff event." Sawyer smiled and shook his head at the memory. "People fanned themselves and swayed like they might faint."

"I bet," Holly said. "Dude, he's the Taylor Swift of the true-crime world right now. It's not every day a serial killer is discovered, and it's even rarer when their child is the one to bring them down. Dude is living his badass era. Did you attend his event? Oh, did you meet him? What was he like? Did he give new details about discovering his dad's crimes or how he decided to go to the police?" Holly didn't fan herself, and she didn't sway on her feet, but she was fangirling so hard that Sawyer wasn't sure where to start.

"Alec was swamped from the moment they announced his name. He took part in several panels, he hosted a meet and greet for the VIP attendees, and he sat for a long book signing." Sawyer cocked a smile. "I bought a book and got it signed for you."

"Shut up!" Holly swatted at his arm. "No, you didn't."

"I did."

"Thank you so much," Holly said. "I can't wait to read it."

"I downloaded the audiobook and listened to it on the way home. There's a lot of information in there about their family dynamics that didn't come out during the trial. And since Alec narrated it himself, I felt like I was sitting across from him and having a conversation over coffee." Sawyer's lips curved into a wicked smile. "And maybe that's because I had a private conversation with him over coffee this week, so I know what it's like."

Holly looked out the window to where Royce stood at the grill. "Does he know?"

Sawyer laughed. "Of course. He didn't enjoy hearing about it, and he disliked the topic of conversation even less."

"Can you share it with me?" Holly formed prayer hands and made big eyes at him.

He shook his head at her antics. "I wouldn't have brought it up otherwise," Sawyer said. "Alec asked to speak to me after I gave my presentation on solving cold cases. He told me that his family had lived in Savannah years ago."

"Really?"

"Yeah, he wants to know if we have unsolved crimes from those years that match his father's MO."

Holly's mouth fell open in surprise, but she snapped it shut. "Seriously?"

"Mm-hmm. Alec doesn't think we've learned the names of all his father's victims, and he doesn't think his dad waited until he was forty years old before he killed for the first time."

"And Andrew can't talk because he died in prison," Holly said.

"Alec introduced me to a woman named Marina Woods, who is going to produce an investigative podcast for him. He has a lot of funding and resources and name recognition. This could be a huge deal."

"His father was a long-haul truck driver," Holly said. "He had access to limitless victims in every state except for Alaska and Hawaii."

"Andrew lived in Alaska for a few years after he divorced Alec's mom," Sawyer told her. "He wanted to try his hand at ice road trucking."

"Wow."

"So there's no telling the true number of victims, and Alec said he won't rest until he finds as many of them as he can."

Holly placed both hands on her chest. "Bless his heart."

"Uh-oh," Jace said. "This doesn't sound good for you, Ro."

"Me?" Royce asked. "They're talking about your unfortunate ass."

Sawyer and Holly turned and found the brothers watching them suspiciously from the open doorway.

"I came back for the cheese." Royce walked into the kitchen with Jace following.

Sawyer pointed to the open sliding glass door, and Holly rolled her eyes in commiseration. "Heathens," she whispered.

"I'm not sure what I just interrupted," Royce said. "Whose foolish heart are you blessing?" He hooked his thumb in his brother's direction just as Jace nodded his head at Royce.

"I didn't use the sarcastic heart blessing," Holly replied. "Sawyer was just telling me about Alec Bishop's mission to uncover as many of his dad's victims as possible."

The Locke brothers groaned in unison and exchanged disgruntled grimaces.

"I'm really sick of hearing about that guy," Jace grumbled.

"At least Holly didn't spend the week with him in Denver," Royce countered.

Sawyer rolled his eyes heavenward for help. "I didn't spend the week with *him*. We were at the same conference and talked a few times."

"One of the conversations was during a private breakfast," Royce told his brother.

"Dude." Jace cast a disappointed look at Sawyer.

"It was in an empty ballroom, not a hotel room, and we weren't alone," Sawyer argued. "His publicist, an agent, and the producer for an upcoming project were also there. We talked about solving cold cases and the possibility that his father could've killed women in Savannah during the mid-nineties."

"Whoa," Jace said. "Seriously?"

Sawyer nodded. "They lived in a rural area in Chatham County but spent a lot of time in Savannah, though I'm not sure how strong Alec's memories are because he was only five at the time."

"So, what's going to happen next?" Holly asked.

"He's probably moving to Savannah for a while to 'investigate' alongside our spouses." Royce's use of air quotes was a nice touch. Sawyer studied his husband closely. Royce hadn't sounded upset when he'd told him about the meeting. Had Sawyer been wrong, or did he just want to wind everyone up? Royce gave him a subtle wink, and Sawyer got his answer.

"Over my dead body," Jace growled.

"Interfere in my career and I just might make that a reality," Holly warned him. "I have loved you since before I even knew what the emotion was, Jace. I don't have the hots for Alec Bishop, but I respect him for turning in his dad and getting justice for the victims' families. The guy didn't just send Andrew to prison. He upended his entire world to do the right thing, which turned his life into a media frenzy."

"One that has paid him handsomely," Jace said. "I bet he's making a fortune off the book he wrote."

"I don't want him or his potential fortune." Holly's mouth curved into a devious smile. "And besides, I'm pretty sure Sawyer is more his type than I am."

And just like that, the glee in Royce's sexy gray eyes dimmed. Jace burst into laughter and teased his brother mercilessly while Sawyer scowled at Holly. "You little minx. I might just use your signed book to start a fire in the pit tonight."

She threw up her hands. "I'm just getting even with Ro for stirring up trouble." Holly turned to Sawyer. "Is Alec really coming here?"

"We're going to look through our cold case database and note any murders that might match Andrew's MO during the times they were in

42

Savannah. I'm going to call Chief Mendoza and Abe this week and see what they think. There's so much media attention on everything Alec does, and we won't want to bring that kind of pressure to our doorsteps unless we're certain we're going on more than wild speculation."

"What about bringing Jonah in to assist?" Holly said.

Stella, the supercomputer Jonah built for the Georgia Bureau of Investigation, would analyze the cold cases much quicker than they could. "I mentioned that to Alec, and he doesn't have hesitations about working with the GBI, but Jonah's side hustle is a concern," Sawyer said.

The idea to start the *Sinister in Savannah* podcast occurred during a poker game at Sawyer and Royce's house. Jonah, Felix, and Rocky couldn't be more different individually, but together, the steadfast GBI agent, dogged reporter, and the wily private investigator formed a tenacious trio. They'd investigated and solved cases that righted decades-old injustices and garnered international attention. Their podcast continued to top the charts years later, and Alec didn't want to tread on their territory. Sawyer suspected he worried more about the trio sweeping in to do their own investigation, and his assurances to the contrary would hold very little sway with Alec since they were virtual strangers.

"He doesn't want to share the limelight," Jace said.

"Maybe," Royce replied. "But the investigation and future podcast are really personal to Alec. I can't fault him for being protective of his intellectual property and wanting to control the narrative."

Sawyer glanced out the window and saw the trio of trouble lounging by the pool with their spouses. A potential connection between Andrew Bishop and Savannah would make them salivate, but they'd never act in a dishonorable way. But he'd honor Alec's wishes and not divulge any parts of their conversation with the podcasters. "This conversation stays between us, right?"

"Like I'd blow an opportunity to get in on this action," Holly said.

Royce gave him the "You have to ask?" look, which drew a wink from Sawyer.

Jace formed a triangle with his fingers and held it above his head. "Cone of silence." He lowered his arms and cocked his head to the side. "Unless I catch that man moving in on my wife. Then all bets are off."

Royce laughed, and Holly rolled her eyes.

"Better get the cheese and get back to the grill before you burn the burgers," Sawyer said.

Royce tsked and shook his head. "Ye of little faith. I've got Diego covering the grill for me." But he pecked a kiss on Sawyer's cheek and retrieved the plate of cheese.

"Why not just leave the cheese platter next to the veggies?" Holly asked. "That way, people can choose their own."

Royce looked at his childhood friend in disbelief. "It's like you've never eaten here before, Holl. Your method won't produce perfectly melted cheese. I'll ask who's eating a burger and what kind of cheese they want so they get a customized experience." Royce pointed in Sawyer's direction. "It's his fancy-ass-foodie influence."

"Guilty as charged." Sawyer would take the blame for this all day, every day. When he'd met Royce, his idea of quality cheese came in a spray can. Sawyer had yet to fully break him of that bad habit, but Royce reached for bougie cheese more often these days. With any luck, the spray imitation cheese would be a thing of the past long before their baby was old enough to enjoy solid foods. Sawyer had to bite back a smile when he thought of the dustups they'd have over nutrition in the years to come.

Once Jace and Royce left, Holly turned to him with a gorgeous smile on her face. "Are we the luckiest people on Earth or what?"

"Yes, we are."

Through the window, he heard Royce calling out to their guests to get their burger orders, which meant it was almost showtime. He and Holly finished putting the toppings platter together before arranging the food, condiments, plates, and cutlery. Their kitchen island made a perfect buffet, and Sawyer stood back with pride once they finished. Holly snagged a piece of pineapple before following Sawyer outside. Those who'd been in the water were toweling off or dripping onto those who'd been lounging poolside.

"Parents with small children get to go first," Royce said.

Jude nudged Felix and said, "That's us."

Royce snorted rudely. "Men with childish husbands don't count."

"Damn it," Jude said. "Maybe we should expand our family with children instead of adding to your flock of peacocks."

"First, we only have one peacock," Felix said. "We have two females, and they're called peahens. We have a *muster* of peafowl."

"Thanks for the lesson, David Attenborough," Royce said. "You still don't get to eat first."

"And," Felix said, holding up a hand, "I don't seek the peafowl; they find me."

"Penelope didn't just show up at our house one day after hearing Pete's and Pearl's squawking," Jude countered. "You'll never convince me that's true no matter how many times you tell the story."

Felix shook his head. "They don't squawk, and I am telling you that Penelope was just there one day after work."

"When I happened to be out of town," Jude teased.

Sawyer leaned toward Royce. "Are they fighting?"

"Foreplay," Royce replied with a wink. The couple was notorious for using witty banter as foreplay. "For fuck's sake, you can get in line with the kids if it will shut you both up."

Jude and Felix smugly fist-bumped one another and joined the line. Sawyer and Royce waited until everyone else cycled through before making their plates. They'd set up folding tables and chairs in long rows on the patio so everyone could gather in one place. Conversation and compliments flowed freely as the large group enjoyed the perfect weather and one another's company. The pool party turned into yard games while they waited for their food to digest so they could return to the water. Sawyer was content to cradle a sleeping Harper against his chest and watch everyone else while Royce turned the carefree games into feisty tournaments.

Felix's phone rang just as Royce launched a cornhole bag at the board. His throw arced right, and the bag landed beside the board instead of on it or through it. Royce cried foul and demanded a do-over as Felix frowned down at his phone.

"No way," Jude told Royce.

"Oh, let the crybaby have it," Felix said as he stepped away to answer his phone.

"I don't need your charity to win," Royce called out.

"Great," Jude said. "It's my turn, then."

The trash talking grew more robust, but something about Felix's posture during the conversation grabbed Sawyer's attention. He stiffened and looked around the party to locate his podcast partners. Rocky and Jonah started moving toward Felix before he'd even disconnected the call, and the trio moved off to the side to have a private chat once he did.

"What do you think that's about?" Holly asked from the chair beside Sawyer.

"Nothing good," he replied. The words were barely out of his mouth when Royce's phone rang. "Told you."

When the Explorer's academic year ended, Chief Mendoza put Royce wherever he needed him most, which usually involved high-profile cases. Felix split his attention between his partners and Royce, whose tense posture said his party had ended. Royce searched the gathering as he spoke until his gaze landed on Diego, who was too busy playing badminton to realize his party was about to end too.

"I'll take back my little man so you can go see what's up," Holly said.

Sawyer carefully transferred the sleeping baby back to his mother before standing up. Royce disconnected his call and looked at him with so much regret in his eyes. It was part of their jobs, and they both knew it. Sawyer darted a glance in Felix's direction and noted that all three podcasters were watching Royce. He tilted his head in their direction and said, "Might want to check with Felix before you take off. I think he got a similar call to yours."

"I figured as much." Royce rested his hand on Sawyer's hip and leaned closer. "Did you see the medical journal on the coffee table at the fertility clinic yesterday?"

"I saw it but paid little attention to it. Did you?"

Royce nodded. "The cover featured a renowned doctor in the fertility field named Jean Claude Matisse. The caption under the photo referred to him as a trailblazer in the field."

"Okay. And…" Sawyer prodded.

"He was just found dead in his swimming pool," Royce replied.

Sawyer furrowed his brow in confusion. "A suspicious death?" It was the only logical reason the chief had called Royce, who worked homicides before becoming the Explorer Academy's director.

"Too soon to tell," Royce replied. "It's an unattended death, and the man has a lot of clout, so Commissioner Rigby has requested my participation, and Mendoza let me choose my partner from the major crimes squad." He sighed heavily and forced his shoulders to relax. "Let's go find out what Felix knows before I ruin Diego's night."

CHAPTER FOUR

ONLY A FEW YEARS AGO, ROYCE WOULD'VE APPROACHED THE situation with Felix a lot differently. Law enforcement agencies and reporters often disagreed about how and when crime should be reported, leading to contentious interactions. Royce had believed journalists only cared about being the first to break the news and make the biggest splash without regard for the victims' families or the investigation. He'd painted Felix with the same broad stroke as all the others. Sawyer hadn't been the reporter's biggest fan either after Felix ran a series of articles exposing the previous Chatham County sheriff's homophobic views. Sawyer's very public exit from the sheriff's department had been a topic in a series of exposés Felix published about CCSD's hostile work environment under Wheeler's leadership, and the wording made it seem like Sawyer had been the reporter's confidential source. Sawyer had taken a lot of heat from his previous colleagues at CCSD and struggled to find acceptance with his new ones at SPD. And by that, Royce meant himself because everyone else had liked Sawyer immediately. Their mutual animosity toward Felix had been something Royce and Sawyer had bonded over in the early days of their professional partnership.

But the intrepid reporter had won their trust and respect over time and had become a valued friend, and Felix proved the feelings were mutual when he tilted his head toward the house to request a private discussion instead of trying to dodge them. Royce could've chased him down, thanks to Sawyer's clean-eating and fitness influence, but he was more than happy to have a simple conversation and reserve his energy. When Rocky and Jonah fell into step behind Felix, Royce realized the news of Dr. Matisse's death likely had a bigger implication than Commissioner Rigby or Chief Mendoza realized. The trio of trouble were already huddled together in the kitchen for a hushed conversation by the time Royce and Sawyer stepped into the house. Royce hadn't caught a word they'd said, but their combined shock and frustration forged a frenetic energy palpable enough to have its own heartbeat. Dread wrapped its gnarled fingers around Royce's heart and squeezed. Dr. Matisse was likely the subject of a *Sinister in Savannah* podcast investigation, and any hope for a swift resolution died right then. The huddle expanded to include Royce and Sawyer as they approached. The trio wore resigned expressions on their faces, but tension tightened the areas around their eyes and bracketed their mouths. They were going to cooperate, but they didn't like it.

Royce crossed his arms over his chest. "Tell me what you know as quickly as you can. I need to grab Diego and head over to the good doctor's house." Royce had used the "good doctor" phrase to get a reaction from his friends, and they didn't disappoint him. Jonah snorted, and Rocky rolled his eyes, but Felix had the most visceral response.

"Good doctor, my ass." Felix practically spat the words, and fire blazed in his gaze. "He was a fucking monster who escaped justice before we could serve it up to him."

"Unless someone beat us to it," Rocky added, turning to Royce.

"Felix's source only told him that Dr. Matisse was found dead in his pool. Did he die from natural causes, or did he have help?"

"I know nothing more than Felix does at the moment." A bitter truth Royce struggled to swallow. Felix's source either worked for SPD or owned a police scanner. It was completely unacceptable for a reporter to receive the information before the lead detective did. But Royce needed Felix's cooperation, so finding out why the doctor's death was important to Felix mattered more than who'd told him. "You're obviously investigating Dr. Matisse for your podcast. Tell me why someone would want to kill him." Royce looked at his watch. "And give me the two-minute-trailer version instead of a lengthy synopsis."

Jonah and Rocky turned to Felix, signaling for him to take the lead. A muscle flexed in the reporter's clenched jaw as he met Royce's gaze. Felix quirked a brow with a silent question he didn't need to ask.

"Yes, you'll be the first to know details of my investigation once it's safe to release them." Royce circled his hand rapidly to urge Felix along.

"The three of us were about to expose fraudulent insemination practices carried out by Jean Claude Matisse over the past four decades," Felix said. "He's operated fertility clinics in several states and used his sperm to inseminate patients without their knowledge or consent."

The words struck Royce like a sucker punch to the gut, knocking the breath from his lungs. Sawyer placed his hand at the small of Royce's back, and they exchanged a quick glance. Of course he'd land a case involving a fertility doctor the day after their own insemination process. He conjured up an image of Dr. Flores' kind face and thought about her professional and compassionate demeanor. Nothing about her had triggered alarms for him. But Dr. Matisse's victims probably felt the same way. *Alleged victims.* He couldn't just accept Felix's statement as fact without more information. Royce pulled air into his lungs and forced himself to focus on the situation at hand instead of making it personal. Which meant he didn't meet his husband's eyes when he felt Sawyer's gaze on him.

"There's so much to unpack here," Royce said. "How do you know this?"

"Genealogy testing," Rocky replied. "People are fascinated by their ancestry. Those kits are popular holiday gifts, and we know of several instances where kids used them for class genealogy projects."

"And suddenly, you have people matching to unknown half siblings all over the country and not sharing genetic markers with the paternal family members they grew up with," Jonah said. "There are forty-eight of his children living in Georgia alone."

"Christ," Sawyer muttered.

"So, these people share a father, but how do you know Matisse is the donor?" Royce asked. "Surely he wasn't stupid enough to submit his DNA to these genealogy sites if he'd fraudulently swapped out the intended donor sperm with his own."

"These siblings started communicating through email, and a pattern immediately formed," Felix explained. "Many of them knew their mothers had undergone fertility treatments to get pregnant with them. Other siblings learned the truth after some tough conversations with their families. Dr. Matisse was the fertility specialist who helped them all."

"And so I *legally* collected the doctor's DNA sample when the guy left an empty smoothie cup sitting on a picnic table at the park," Rocky said. "We paid for the DNA test ourselves and hired an expert to do the DNA comparisons. We wanted irrefutable proof, and we got it. I am one thousand percent sure this man lied to his patients when he claimed he'd used their husband's or chosen donor's sperm."

Royce turned to look at his husband for the first time since the conversation started. They'd been riding an emotional high since leaving the fertility clinic the previous day, even though they knew success wasn't guaranteed. That same optimism shimmered in Sawyer's chocolate-brown eyes, but caution tempered it now. Royce wanted the unbridled joy back for both of them. He wanted to assure Sawyer that everything would be okay. Hell, he wanted the guarantee too. But that was a private conversation they'd have later. Royce had pressing work to do, so he forced his attention back to their friends.

"It sounds like you've been investigating Dr. Matisse for a while," Royce said.

"Almost a year," Felix replied. "The forty-eight local families are just the tip of the iceberg."

"Sounds like an expensive investigation," Sawyer said.

Felix nodded. "Very, but we didn't do this alone. When we realized the scope of the investigation, we sought partnerships with *Savannah Morning News* and Channel Eleven. In return for their investment, I am publishing an exposé in the Sunday edition. Jude is to follow up with reporting for Channel Eleven on Sunday evening. The podcast will handle the long-form investigation with weekly episode drops, starting on Monday. We will provide occasional updates to our news affiliate partners and provide them with bonus content they could tuck behind paywalls to generate revenue. We recorded most of the episodes already, but it's still an active investigation."

"Especially now that Matisse is dead," Rocky said.

Royce glanced at the time on the microwave and winced. They'd far exceeded the two-minute mark, and he still needed to change his clothes and inform Diego that his party was over. "How'd you become involved with the siblings?"

"Dr. Matisse's last clinic was in Savannah, and he retired here. His local victims are aware of our podcast and reached out because the doctor's behavior was downright sinister," Felix explained.

"Why not pursue legal or civil action?" Sawyer asked.

"Statutes of limitations prevent the victims from legal recourse, but I expect a civil suit is forthcoming. They wanted to focus on exposing his misdeeds first."

"Does Dr. Matisse know what you've uncovered?" Royce asked.

Felix nodded. "It's unethical for me to run a hit piece without giving him an opportunity to respond to the allegations. I called his home around noon on Friday, and we had a brief conversation. He denied any wrongdoing and refused to comment further. Dr. Matisse referred all future questions to his legal counsel but refused to name a lawyer or provide their contact information when I asked for it."

Royce heaved a sigh. "That'll have to be enough for now, but I'm holding you to this agreement."

"As long as you keep your end of the bargain," Felix replied.

Royce turned to Sawyer. They both knew the hazards of being law enforcement officers and the toll it took on their private life, so there was no need to apologize. He did it anyway. "I'm sorry this ruined our plans. I'll get back as fast as I can."

"I know you will."

They shared a brief kiss before Royce left him in the kitchen to retrieve his temporary partner. Diego smiled as he approached, but his good humor faded when he clocked Royce's expression.

"No, man," Diego groaned. "Come on, Ro."

"Chief Mendoza has tagged me to work a high-profile case, and I've chosen you to be my partner."

Diego gestured to his board shorts and lifted his discarded T-shirt off the lounger. "You expect me to go to a crime scene dressed like this?"

Levi leaned over and kissed his husband's cheek. "There's a go bag for you in the trunk of my car."

Diego narrowed his eyes, and his lips formed a little pout. "Sounds like you're eager to get rid of me."

Levi rolled his eyes and nudged him with his shoulder. There was a significant size difference between the husbands, so Levi's gesture barely budged Diego. "I just know how these things go."

"Grab your things and get changed." Royce gestured to himself. "I'll do the same, and we'll meet out front."

"I'll be there," Diego said dryly.

Sawyer was sitting on the bed when Royce reached their room. "The universe isn't sending me a message, right?" Sawyer had lived another life before meeting Royce. He'd been married and happily in love with Victor Ruiz, and they'd been approved for adoption right before Vic received a terminal cancer diagnosis. The situations were in no way similar, but would Felix's bombshell trigger fears that Sawyer had hoped to leave in the past? Did he feel like his dreams of fatherhood were on the verge of being yanked away again?

Royce shut the door and inhaled a deep, slow breath. The long exhale acted like a reset button for his brain. Sawyer's soulful eyes implored Royce to give him promises he had no business making. He crossed the room to stand before Sawyer, who stood up so they were eye to eye. "Dr. Flores is not Dr. Matisse. She is a brilliant, kind doctor who has dedicated her life to making dreams like ours come true."

"All the mothers who'd visited Dr. Matisse's clinics probably thought the same thing. You and I both know how heightened emotions interfere with perception and judgment. We weren't utilizing our specialized training during our interactions at the clinic. We were firing on hopes, dreams, and adrenaline. We were just as vulnerable as anyone else in those moments."

Royce cupped Sawyer's face. "I have enough faith for both of us. Our insemination was successful, and we're going to have a baby.

Probably a little girl who will have us wrapped around her finger before she draws her first breath. Anytime doubt tries to wiggle in, just think about that."

Sawyer wrapped his arms around Royce and held on for dear life. "We're going to have a baby."

"Damn right, we are." And no deviant doctor's past deeds would ruin this beautiful journey for them.

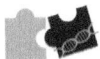

"That's fucked-up," Diego said as they sped toward the Oaks, an exclusive gated community. "And it sounds like there will be a lot of suspects if his death resulted from foul play."

"And more media coverage than we can imagine." Royce lifted his left hand off the steering wheel and crossed his fingers. "Please let it be natural causes."

"Amen," Diego agreed. "Have you told Mendoza what you learned from Felix and the gang?" Everyone had a different nickname for the trio of trouble. Some sounded like rock bands, others like motorcycle gangs, and one made Royce think of a softball team. Felix was the ringleader in every scenario, and it was a badge of honor he wore proudly.

"Not yet," Royce replied as he pulled to a stop at a red light. "I wanted to wait until we've assessed the situation. Telling Mendoza now would take things from a ten to a hundred."

"I'll trust your instincts," Diego said. "But I won't hesitate to throw you under the bus if the chief demands to know why we waited to tell him about the fraud allegations."

Royce looked over at his temporary partner. "Message received."

"It'll look like this." Diego widened his brown eyes and let his mouth go slack. He blinked rapidly and snapped his mouth shut. "Chief, I had no idea. This is the first I'm hearing about the allegations."

The performance deserved a slow clap, and Royce gave him one before returning his attention to the traffic light. "Mendoza would see through that bullshit in a nanosecond." The light turned green, and Royce accelerated through the intersection.

"Too much?"

"I think it was the unhinged jaw trick," Royce told him. "And maybe you were too breathy. Less of a seductress next time. But the anime eyes were pretty good though. I thought I saw tears of betrayal trembling on your ridiculous eyelashes."

"Hey! My lashes are ridiculously long, but they're *not* ridiculous." Diego's genuine outrage made Royce laugh. "And I'll have you know that these bad boys get me out of a lot of trouble at home."

"Yeah, D," Royce said dryly. "It's your eyelashes that Levi can't resist."

"Well, he likes other things too."

Diego was a hunk of a man, so there were limitless physical attributes for his husband to admire. But the guy was a genuinely wonderful person, which made him even more attractive. That's why Royce had loathed him on sight years ago, when he'd been fighting his feelings for Sawyer. Diego had swept in with his swarthy good looks and open admiration for the man Royce had wanted but was afraid to claim. But Diego's challenge wasn't the one that had pushed Royce to make his move. That honor belonged to Levi, who'd actually gone on a date with Sawyer and forced Royce to acknowledge his feelings. In fact, it was Royce's petty insecurities that made him push Levi in Diego's path. He'd just wanted to distract both men from their attraction to Sawyer, and they'd ended up falling in love and getting married.

Royce slowed as they approached their destination. "Your dimples, right?"

"Yeah, but which set?"

He glanced over at the passenger seat as he turned into a gated neighborhood. Diego winked and nearly blinded him with his white smile. "That's a mystery I don't need to solve."

A pristine white sign nestled amidst colorful flowers and lush shrubs announced they'd reached the Oaks with pretentious gold lettering. Royce nearly sprained his eyeballs rolling them. He was grateful they didn't get stuck in the back of his head when the guardhouse came into view. The structure was supposed to look like a miniature version of a grandiose house you'd find behind the gates, but the designer had failed epically. "I get what they were going for," Royce said, "but that thing looks like an oversized kids' dollhouse."

Diego cackled beside him. "It reminds me of my niece's Little Tikes playhouse."

Royce forced back a laugh when he pulled to a stop at the shack. Both he and Diego lifted their badges for inspection. The security guard was young and looked visibly shaken. His voice cracked, and it took him two tries to give them directions to the Matisses' house. "Thank you," Royce said before accelerating through the open gate. "That was much better than the last time I was in a community like this." As he navigated the winding roads, he told Diego about the time he and Sawyer got pulled over by a glorified mall cop driving a souped-up golf cart.

"I guess it's good that they take their jobs so seriously, but they don't have more authority over us in any situation," Diego said.

"I set Paul Blart straight that day."

"That's a movie I haven't seen in ages," Diego said.

They shared a few movie quotes as they navigated through the sprawling community. The estates were built on large lots, probably three- to five-acre tracts because there weren't many homes on each street.

"Here we go," Royce said when they reached the Matisses' mailbox.

Their residence was the last property on a dead-end road. The driveway was so long and the surrounding trees so dense that they didn't see the emergency vehicles until the house came into view. Pea gravel turned into ornate brick pavers the closer they got to the home. The parking area was enormous enough to accommodate a white Lexus, two SPD patrol cars, an ambulance, the crime scene techs, and the medical examiner's van. Royce parked behind the Lexus and removed two sets of latex gloves and disposable booties from his glove box before they got out of his SUV.

The back doors of the ambulance were open, and there was a flurry of activity inside. A woman with wet, reddish-blonde hair plastered to her head sat on the gurney with an emergency blanket draped around her shoulders like a cape. Her yellow sundress was soaked and clinging to her trembling body. She wore a white sandal on one pale foot, but the other was bare. Royce figured she'd gone into the pool to give Dr. Matisse aid and lost a shoe at some point. Was she his daughter? His wife? An employee?

The mournful wail of a wounded animal tore from her throat, and the two female EMTs kneeled on either side of the gurney to comfort her. Perla and Lydia were two of the city's finest first responders, and Royce respected them immensely. They were fierce and fearless whenever the situation called for it but always compassionate when dealing with traumatized people like the woman clutching the Mylar blanket with a fist.

"I c-c-can't believe this," she stuttered. "He's the h-h-healthiest person I know. This c-c-can't be real."

Lydia looked up when Royce and Diego approached the back of

the ambulance. She'd dyed her close-cropped hair a rose-gold color that contrasted prettily with her ebony skin and hazel eyes. Lydia greeted Royce with a sad smile, and he tilted his head to the right, requesting a private conversation. She patted the woman's knee and told her she'd be right back, which prompted her to lift her head to see where Lydia was going. Bloodshot eyes met his, but it was the icy blue color of her irises that snagged his attention.

Royce had seen the same hue in the photograph of Dr. Matisse on the magazine cover, though their expression couldn't have been more different. Dr. Matisse had come across as cold and arrogant where this woman, most likely his daughter, was devastated. Little did she know, things were about to get even worse for her. There was no way Felix would pull his punches in the wake of the doctor's death. The story would break exactly as he'd intended, shoving Royce and Diego into the spotlight too. The pressure to find a swift resolution would be insane, and their every move would be scrutinized to the nth degree. They'd have to toe the line or walk the plank of public scrutiny. And no matter the outcome of their investigation, someone would be angry and very vocal with their dissent. Royce would likely see vastly different expressions in this woman's eyes over the next coming days, and he'd have to adjust his demeanor accordingly. But right then, she was a heartbroken woman who deserved his compassion.

"Ma'am," Royce said. "I'm Sergeant Locke, and this is Detective Fuentes. We're very sorry for your loss."

"Th-th-thank you. I'm Ju-julia Matisse," she stammered. "Detective?" Her voice sounded raspy, and Julia pressed a delicate hand to her throat and swallowed hard.

"Do you need a drink?" Perla asked.

She nodded. "Please."

Perla retrieved a bottle of water from deeper inside the ambulance and uncapped it for her. Julia thanked her and took several drinks before attempting to speak again.

"I thought they only sent detectives to murder scenes," Julia said.

"We respond to many calls, including unattended deaths," Royce explained. "I'm here as a personal favor to Commissioner Rigby." Delicately winged brows arched upward. Royce wasn't sure if she knew Rigby personally or if she was confused about why a highly ranked police official would get involved. He could find that out later. She was shivering from head to toe in her wet dress.

"Can you tell us what happened?" Royce asked gently.

Julia nodded. "I'm here visiting my family for the holiday weekend. We were all supposed to attend a party at our friends' house, but Father never showed." Her lips trembled, and she pressed her fingers against her mouth to stop them. After a few seconds, she lowered her hand and continued speaking. "I called his cell phone and the house line, but he didn't answer. Our house staff was already gone for the weekend, so there was no one to check on him. I drove back here and found him…found him in the…" She shook her head as sobs racked her body. "I can't say it. Then it's real."

"She's had quite a shock," Lydia said gently. "Do you mind if she changes into something warm and dry?"

"Of course not," Royce replied. "I need to start my preliminary investigation at the pool, so take your time. I'd like to interview you afterward if you're up to it."

Julia nodded jerkily. "Of course. I'll help however I can."

"Where would you feel most comfortable talking to us?"

Julia told them she preferred to meet in her mother's salon and gave them directions to find the room when they were ready.

"Thank you," Royce said. "Can we access the pool by walking around the house, or should we go through it?"

"There is an access gate in the fence, but I don't know the electric code. The house is unlocked, so you can go straight through to the back."

"We'll talk soon." Royce gestured for Diego to precede him. He'd wanted to talk to Lydia about her observations when she first arrived, but it would have to wait until they could speak privately.

They stopped on the porch and slipped on their booties. A massive set of wood double doors stood open, and they stepped over the threshold. The interior of the Matisse home was as stately as the exterior, with luxurious attention given to every detail. White marble flooring stretched endlessly ahead of them, and intricately carved pillars towered two stories high in the grand foyer. A mural painted on the cathedral ceiling featured curly-haired cherubs peeking over the edge of fluffy white clouds dotting a blue sky. Royce stopped suddenly and stared up at the ceiling, wondering if there was a deeper meaning behind the winged babies depicted in the painting. The cherubs' expressions ranged from innocent to impish. They each wore a different wreath of flowers on their heads, and the positioning of the crowns matched their expressions. The innocent-looking cherubs wore a straight wreath, where the flower crowns on the mischievous ones sat askew. The details were so lifelike that it gave the appearance that the little darlings were watching them. Royce halfway expected their eyes to follow them once they started moving again.

"This reminds me of the show at Caesar's Palace in Las Vegas but without the giant talking statues," Diego said. "I'm running the hell out of here if the clouds move and the cherubs giggle."

Royce slapped Diego's shoulder. "Let's go." He darted a glance upward and was relieved to note the cherubs were not tracking their movements.

CHAPTER FIVE

ROYCE ASSESSED THE ROOMS AS THEY MOVED TOWARD THE REAR of the residence, but he didn't find obvious signs of distress or disturbance, only the occasional puddle of water Julia had tracked inside. The house seemed too sterile to be inhabited. Everything was pristine and elegantly displayed, resembling a model home instead of a gathering place for family. Not a discarded pair of shoes kicked off after someone entered a room or a forgotten empty glass left on a table. Sawyer was the tidiest person Royce had ever met, but he was a slob compared to these people. Every clutter-free surface gleamed, stirring within Royce an irrational need to make a mess. Seriously, no coffeepot or canisters? No keys or mail haphazardly tossed on the island as someone passed through? Who were these people?

The rear of the house featured a wall of windows that overlooked the pool and a meticulously landscaped backyard beyond it. Royce halted mid-step to take in the stunning flora and fauna stretching for probably an acre. Lush blooms and neatly trimmed shrubs had been arranged by color and height in the most dazzling display Royce had ever seen. A paver walking path divided the sections and led to a large water fountain in the center, where a six-foot curvaceous goddess rose from the water. She held a bouquet in her hands, and water spilled from a large, overturned vase at her feet.

"There's your talking statue," Royce said.

"Nah, we've gone from Caesar's Palace to the set of *Bridgerton*," Diego said.

Movement on the far right of the patio caught Royce's attention. Dr. Fawkes, the medical examiner, used a pool skimmer to guide Dr. Matisse's body closer to the edge of the pool, where her assistants waited with outstretched hands to grip him. The deceased was tall and muscular and would not be easy to get out of the water. Officers Howard East and Erica Black were on the scene too, though neither of them seemed eager to help. Royce nudged Diego with his elbow and tilted his head to the struggling medical examiner's team. He slipped on his first glove and said, "Shall we?"

Diego sighed and pulled his gloves on too. "If we must." They continued through the house and stepped onto the patio. The patrol officers turned at their approach and exchanged a surprised glance amongst themselves when they saw who'd responded.

East, a transplant from Boston with the build and countenance of a bulldog, spoke first. "Sending out the big guns, huh?" He flexed his arm and pointed at his biceps straining his uniform.

Black, a petite Asian woman, rolled her eyes at her partner's antics. "At first glance, this death looks like an open-shut case." She gestured at a patio table where two crime scene techs were looking at an empty crystal decanter and a pill bottle. "Benzodiazepines and booze."

Royce and Diego walked over to the table and waited for the techs to photograph and document the scene before examining the evidence. The prescription was for Alyssa Matisse and had been filled two days prior. The instructions said for her to take two to three pills per day as needed for anxiety, and the bottle was still pretty full. "Dr. Fawkes will do her best to determine how many of these he ingested," Royce said to Diego. He gestured to the empty crystal decanter and matching glass. "And how much of this he consumed." Royce removed the stopper from the decanter and lifted it to his nose. "Scotch. And it smells very expensive." He set it down and gestured to the pool where Fawkes and her team were preparing to remove Dr. Matisse from the water.

"Let us give you a hand," Royce called out.

Dr. Fawkes looked over her shoulder and sighed with relief. "Thank you. I didn't want to ask my team to get into the pool with potential contaminants in the water."

Royce concentrated on getting the man out of the pool without causing postmortem injuries that would require lengthy reports. He looked over his shoulder at East and Black. "Hey, can you guys move the body bag closer and hold it still so it won't shift?" The officers exchanged a weary look but moved into position and did what he asked. Five of them carefully removed the dead man from the pool and set him on top of the black body bag.

Fawkes fixed Royce with a shrewd gaze. "I'm surprised to see you here."

"I could say the same for you, Doc. I'd think you'd have enough clout to take the holiday weekend off."

She offered a weary smile. "I'm here for the same reason you are." She straightened her shoulders and surveyed their elegant surroundings. "Our deceased gentleman must have friends in high places."

"You don't know him?" Royce asked.

She glanced down at the man her technicians were photographing. "Should I?"

"Dr. Jean Claude Matisse," Diego said.

Dr. Fawkes arched a brow. "And you think all doctors know one another? Medical examiners don't get invited to sit at the cool kids' table."

"You can sit with me any day, Doc," Royce told her.

She smiled gently. "Tell me why this doctor is so important."

"He was a renowned fertility specialist in the country," Royce told her. "He last practiced in Savannah and retired here."

"Ahhh." Fawkes nodded her head toward the statue in the water fountain. "She makes more sense now."

"Which goddess is she?" Diego asked.

"Flora," Fawkes replied. "She's a Roman goddess who represents spring, abundance, and fertility."

Royce turned his gaze and scrutinized the garden through a new lens. One might think the doctor had established the colorful, lush plantings as a tribute to the goddess. In a way, the plants almost looked like worshiping servants at her feet. "That's something," he said. Felix would have a field day with this information when Royce could share it. "There's an empty decanter of booze and a prescription for benzodiazepines on the patio table. At first glance, this seems like an overdose, but I'm not sure if it's accidental or intentional." The medical examiner and her investigators would take lead until there was evidence of a crime. Royce was acting as her support at the moment.

"I will put blood, urine, and vitreous humor through my automated immunoanalyzer to get preliminary toxicology reports for drugs and alcohol in his system, but that alone won't tell us if he'd intended to die or got carried away with experimenting."

"How long before we have some answers, Doc?"

"Thirty minutes for the initial drug and alcohol test results, but I need to do a complete autopsy first. I'll try to have preliminary data in twenty-four to thirty-six hours."

"That's much better than waiting two or three months for results to come back from a forensics lab," Royce said.

"I may have to send samples off for additional testing or to double-check ambiguous results. But the toxicology won't be the only factor in my ruling, and I expect Dr. Matisse's body will provide a lot of answers for me." She placed her hands on the small of her back and stretched her spine. "I'll need to review his medical records and talk to his family about his recent state of mind and what was going on in his life. His organ and hair samples will reveal if this is a long-term habit for the doctor or a newer hobby, but I won't have those answers quickly. The crime scene technicians will dust the decanter, glass, and pill bottle for fingerprints. I'll run tests on the contents and residues to see if someone has tampered with them, but—"

"Those results will take time," Royce finished for her.

"Unfortunately." Dr. Fawkes scanned the patio area before meeting Royce's gaze. "Will you send me your interview notes after you speak to the person who found Dr. Matisse? I'll read them after performing the autopsy and will contact the family if I need additional details to determine his cause of death."

"Sure thing," Royce said. "I'll send you my notes right away." He scanned the expanse of the outdoor living space and couldn't find a single shred of evidence pointing to foul play. It was just as pristine as the interior. "Everything is under control here. We'll head back inside and talk to Julia Matisse."

"We'll talk when I know more," Dr. Fawkes said.

Royce and Diego retraced their steps through the house to the midway point, made a left turn down a hallway, and followed the directions Julia had given them to find her mother's salon.

"What's a salon?" Diego whispered.

"It's what French high society called their social gatherings for intellectual conversations."

Diego stopped suddenly, forcing Royce to halt too. "How in the hell do *you* know that?"

66

Royce quirked a brow. "I don't care for your tone, Fuentes."

"You had to learn it from Sawyer," Diego said.

Royce wanted to get angry at his assumption, but everyone knew Sawyer was the intellectual one in their relationship with a law degree from Duke University. If Royce let things like the truth bother him, he'd never be happy. So he shrugged. "My guy loves to watch documentaries about anything and everything." Sniffling came from the room nearest them, and Royce gestured for them to continue. Once they fell into step, he leaned closer and lowered his voice. "I think a salon in this instance is probably a fancy or formal room to gather."

"I thought that was called a parlor."

"I consider them to be the same thing, but I'm sure my super-intelligent husband could tell you the difference."

Diego snorted, but a soft flush crept up his neck. "I didn't mean to imply you're not an intelligent person. I just didn't expect you to come with the French high society facts."

He wanted to tease Diego more about his assumptions and feign wounded pride, but they'd reached their destination, and so his torment would have to wait a little longer. He'd get his revenge when Diego least expected it. They stepped into the salon, which was as formal and feminine as Royce had expected it to be. The teacup rose wallpaper was the focal point of the room, and everything in the space, from fabric colors and textures to the furniture's shape, complemented or matched the wall treatment. Even the massive white fireplace featured elegantly carved rose vines climbing up and across the mantel.

Julia Matisse sat on a pastel green velvet settee, another term Royce had learned from Sawyer, with her legs pulled up to her chest so that only her bare toes peeked out from beneath her flowy pink skirt. She'd wrapped her arms around her legs and pressed her forehead to her knees. Her wet, wavy hair swung forward to hide her face from their view. But soft weeping and trembling shoulders attested to her heartbreak without them seeing her expression. She sniffled again and dabbed at her eyes with a tissue, reminding Royce that he probably had a limited time to get coherent answers from her before she shut down.

Her head snapped up when she heard them approach. Julia's eyes were as red as a person on a three-day bender. They looked as raw as her expression. She sniffed and pulled a fresh tissue from the box on the coffee table. The crumpled one fell forgotten to her lap as she tried to pull herself together. "I'm sorry."

"Don't be," Diego said. "You've had a terrible shock."

"And we're truly sorry for your loss, Miss Matisse," Royce said, then gestured to the pair of chairs across from her. "May we?"

She sniffed and nodded. "And it's Dr. Matisse, but you can call me Julia to minimize confusion."

"Pardon me," Royce said. "Do you mind if I record our conversation so I can refer to it while making my report?"

She shook her head. "Of course not."

Royce pulled up the app and hit Play before setting his phone on the table between them. "This is Sergeant Royce Locke with Detective Diego Fuentes, interviewing Dr. Julia Matisse at the home of her parents, Dr. Jean Claude Matisse and …" He let his voice trail off so she could confirm the bottle outside belonged to her mother.

"Mrs. Alyssa Matisse," Julia supplied for him.

Royce rattled off the date and time before launching into questions. "Can you tell me about your father's day, Julia?"

Her lips trembled, and she pressed the tissue to her mouth before lowering her head. She met his gaze again after a few seconds and swallowed hard. "I can tell you about his day until I left for the Barclays' house for their annual barbecue."

"Mayor Barclay?" Diego asked.

Julia's shoulders stiffened slightly, and she pressed her lips into a firm line. "Yes, but I call him Uncle Elliott."

The reason for their presence became crystal clear. The mayor had likely called Commissioner Rigby and asked for her help. "Were your parents supposed to attend the barbecue as well?"

She nodded, and Royce gently asked her to answer out loud since he was only recording their voices. "Sorry. Yes. Both my parents had planned to attend the barbecue. They'd both mentioned it multiple times since I arrived from Boston on Thursday afternoon." Julia tilted her head and narrowed her eyes slightly. "Well, my mother had mostly steered the conversation about it. My father mentioned the party at dinner on Thursday night but hadn't brought it up since. In fact, he has said very little about anything since Friday afternoon. He'd—" She cut herself off suddenly and shook her head. "You didn't ask about yesterday."

"Please continue," Royce said. "It would be extremely important if you would tell us what you observed about your dad since you arrived in town."

Julia exhaled a deep breath and released it slowly. "Father has never been someone you'd describe as gregarious. He was extremely cerebral and lived mostly in his brain. He was introverted to a point that most would call him socially awkward, but Uncle Elliott always brought out the best in him. Father could let his guard down and enjoy the food, liquor, and company at his gatherings. That's why it was odd when he snapped at Mother for mentioning the barbecue this morning." Julia lowered her head and shredded the tissue in her hand. Was this a sign of agitation or anxiety?

"Was it rare for your father to lose his temper?" Diego asked.

Julia snapped her head back up and pinned Diego with an icy glare. "I didn't say he lost his temper. That was beneath him. Father just got short with Mother when she kept bringing Elliott up in conversation.

Something was clearly bothering him, but she just kept going on about the party. What she was going to wear and how we should dress. He'd just had enough and got snippy with her."

"Can you remember what Dr. Matisse specifically said?" Royce prodded.

Julia closed her eyes and swayed slightly. When she reopened them, she wore a faraway expression. "Father told her to back off and stop nagging him. He had bigger concerns than what to wear to a garden party and didn't want her hounding him. They argued for a few minutes, and Mother stormed from the room. Father closed his eyes and seemed to enjoy the silence until I shattered it."

"How?" Diego asked.

"I dropped a juice glass on the kitchen floor and broke it," Julia said. A look of utter embarrassment washed over her features. Royce figured she was in her late thirties or maybe even in her early forties. It seemed so strange that such a simple accident could cause so much strife. "Father was furious with me and berated me for my clumsy behavior." As if remembering her previous claims, she added, "But he never raised his voice. He didn't need to. His tongue was as sharp as a scalpel and just as deadly." She snapped her mouth shut and pressed her hand to her lips. Julia closed her eyes, and a fresh wave of tears cascaded down her face.

Royce feared they wouldn't get through the interview, but then she straightened her shoulders and said she was ready to continue. "What happened after the incident with the glass?"

"I cleaned it up and got ready for the party. We were all supposed to leave together, but Father had announced at breakfast that he was waiting for an important phone call from his friend, um, his attorney and would drive separately. I asked Mother to join me, but she had hoped to change Father's mind and ride with him. She arrived alone at the party about an hour after I did."

"Was there anyone else in the home that might've witnessed unusual behavior from Dr. Matisse?" Diego asked.

"Yvonne and Ricardo," Julia said absently, then shook her head. "I'm sorry. Yvonne is my parents' housekeeper, and Ricardo is our chef." She narrowed her eyes as if thinking hard. "They left early on Friday to start their holiday weekend, but I don't know the specific time."

"So they don't live on-site?" Royce asked.

"No, they don't. I'm almost positive they left before the fireworks began."

He thought her phrasing was odd. To describe an argument as fireworks implied it had gotten pretty explosive. And Julia had claimed that something bigger had been weighing on Dr. Matisse. Royce knew he was headed into delicate territory and needed to tread lightly. He wanted to find out if she or her mother knew anything about the looming allegations without tipping his hand. "Was it common practice for your father to have a conversation with his attorney on a holiday weekend?"

Julia narrowed her eyes to icy slits. Royce worried he'd gone too far, but she smoothed her expression and took another deep breath. "It's not unusual. My father is—*was*—a demanding man. If he deemed something important, he didn't want to wait until office hours to have a discussion. Considering the amount of money my father has paid Richard Todd over the years, it's not too much to expect a return phone call on a Saturday."

"Do you have any idea what could've been so urgent for your father?" Diego asked.

"No," Julia replied with a sigh. "I tried to press him a little yesterday when I first noticed his mood had soured. He got brusque with me and said I should mind my own business." Her lips trembled for a few seconds before she pressed them together. "I went behind his back and asked Mother about his mood swings, but she denied noticing anything wrong with him." Julia snorted and rolled her eyes. "I'd like to take whatever medication her doctor prescribed her."

"Benzodiazepine," Royce said. "I saw the bottle next to the empty scotch decanter."

Julia's brow furrowed. "What is the prescription used for?"

Royce considered her question for a few seconds. He wasn't a doctor, but he'd heard about benzos. "You're not familiar with the medication as a doctor?"

Julia offered a bless-your-heart smile and said, "I'm not that kind of doctor. I have a PhD in theater, and I work as a director and producer in Boston."

"Your parents must be so proud," Diego said.

She sat as still as a statue while she assessed his remark. Was she looking for sarcasm? Then, as if someone flipped a switch, she went into action again, wringing her hands. "My mother is very proud of me, but my father believes my education and vocation are a complete waste of time, money, and brainpower. He has zero respect for creative arts and believes the only doctors that count are the ones who've completed medical school and the specialized training for their field."

Royce thought her father sounded like a complete asshole, but he tried not to let his expression show that.

Julia pinned him with a penetrative stare. "You don't approve, Sergeant Locke."

Oops. He hadn't suppressed his resting dickhead face quickly enough. "I don't," he admitted. "That isn't the type of father I want to become to my future children."

Genuine approval shone in her eyes. "Then don't."

He took her advice with a soft nod before steering them back to the reason for the conversation. "People often take benzodiazepine for anxiety and depression. Mixing them with alcohol is extremely dangerous and can be deadly."

"And that's what you think happened to my father," Julia said.

"That is the working theory based on the limited evidence available. The medical examiner will investigate to see if there were other contributing factors."

"So, he either accidentally overdosed or…" Her words trailed off as she folded into herself like a crumpled tissue.

"Juju!" a woman yelled from somewhere in the house. "What's going on?"

Julia gasped and bolted to her feet. She ran for the door about the time an older woman with perfectly coiffed platinum blonde hair walked into the room. "Mother!"

Alyssa Matisse wore a white pantsuit with wide, flowy legs that swished when she walked. She must've been in her late sixties or early seventies but looked almost as young as her daughter. Alyssa stopped just shy of Julia's outstretched arms. "Eli broke the news to me, and I insisted he drive me home right away. Tell me it's not true." Dark eyes implored her daughter to allay her fears.

"I'm so sorry, Mother," Julia whispered.

Alyssa shook her head repeatedly, unwilling to believe the truth, but Julia nodded solemnly. The older woman released a keening wail and collapsed into her daughter's waiting arms. "No. I won't believe it."

A silver-haired man entered the salon and assessed the situation with a shrewd, dark gaze. Mayor Barclay took both women into his arms and cradled them against his chest. "I'm so sorry," he told them.

Alyssa pulled back enough to look at Barclay's face. "Did you see Jean Claude? Is it real?"

"Do you think I made the whole thing up?" Julia asked in a clipped voice.

"Of course not," Alyssa said. "This situation is just unfathomable."

"The officers prevented me from walking onto the patio, but I saw enough through the wall of windows to know it's true." Barclay briefly closed his eyes. When he reopened them, his gaze locked on Royce and Diego. He lowered his head and whispered something to the women before he lowered his arms and strode forward. His shoulders rose, and his chest puffed out a little when he reached them. "Who's in charge?"

Royce stuck out his hand. "I'm Sergeant Locke, sir."

The mayor shook his hand and looked to Diego for an introduction. He gestured for Royce to join him for a private conversation, and he obliged the man. "What can you tell me so far?"

"We're still in the preliminary stages of the investigation, but I'd just discussed what evidence we'd found so far with Julia when her mother arrived. If it's okay with them, we can have this discussion together. Maybe you can offer invaluable insight on the situation."

"I can try." He looked over at the women, who huddled together crying. "I'd like to get this over with as quickly as possible tonight. Perhaps we can have a longer discussion tomorrow or Monday. Julia and Alyssa will be overwhelmed with funeral arrangements."

"I understand that, and I will accommodate them as best I can. There are a few more things I need to ask this evening."

"Okay," Barclay said. "Do you mind if I sit in and provide moral support?"

"I'm sure they'd appreciate that," Royce replied.

"I've been like an uncle to Julia." He glanced over at the women again. "More like a father figure, if I'm telling the truth. Jean Claude spent ninety percent of his time ensuring other people achieved their dreams of parenthood and left very little energy for his only daughter.

That didn't change when he retired either. Alyssa and Julia were his accessories and nothing more." He pressed his lips together and shook his head. "Julia has spent her entire life chasing his approval, and now she'll never receive it."

Royce knew Julia's daddy issues were about to get much worse, but he just nodded sagely. He and Barclay returned to the others and sat down. He gestured to his phone and informed them he was recording the conversation. Then he noted the recent additions to the conversation and the time before continuing. "Mrs. Matisse, I need to ask how your husband seemed before you left for Mayor Barclay's house. Julia said he'd been agitated before she left an hour prior."

Alyssa scowled briefly in her daughter's direction. "Jean Claude was just a little out of sorts."

"Mother," Julia chided. "The officers need you to take off your rose-colored glasses where Father is concerned and answer their questions honestly."

"Julia! I think you forget who the parent is here."

"Ladies, please," Barclay cajoled. "This isn't the time to argue. The officers want to figure out what happened to Jean Claude, though I don't know why they're asking about his mood."

"Because Father either accidentally or purposely overdosed on expensive scotch and Mother's antidepressants."

Alyssa gasped and clutched her chest. She sucked in short bursts of air, and Royce worried she'd gone into cardiac arrest until Julia got her to calm down through repetitive breaths, counting for her mother during her inhales and exhales. "Impossible," Alyssa whispered raggedly.

"What's impossible?" Barclay asked.

"He couldn't have mixed my pills and booze," Alyssa said.

"Lyss, people do it all the time." Barclay looked at Royce. "Jean Claude was furious about something yesterday. He phoned me in the afternoon to inquire if Richard Todd would be at the party. That's our mutual friend and Jean Claude's former attorney. I told him that Richard was spending the day with his son's family. That only seemed to irritate Jean Claude more. I asked if there was something I could do to help, but he insisted only Richard would do."

"Does anyone know if Dr. Matisse ever spoke to Richard?" Royce asked.

The three of them shook their heads.

Then Alyssa sniffled delicately. "Jean Claude and I briefly argued after Julia left for Elliott's. I told my husband it was silly to mope around the house like a teenage girl waiting for the phone to ring."

Julia scoffed. "You did not say that, Mother. You never stand up to him."

Alyssa leaned forward to peer around Barclay. "I absolutely did, and those were the last words I said to him." She looked at Royce, her expression somber but determined. "Jean Claude couldn't have taken my prescription pills because he didn't know about them. My husband thinks—" Her words stopped as if abruptly hitting a brick wall. "*Thought*," she said hoarsely. Alyssa paused and closed her eyes. Tears trickled from the corners and ran down her face. She took a few more breaths and met Royce's gaze once more. "Jean Claude thought depression and anxiety were excuses people gave to avoid difficult things."

Royce hazarded a quick glance at Julia in time to catch her subtle flinch before she said, "And he said pharmaceutical companies got rich off making people sick." Julia raised her hands. "Not saying I believe that. I know damn well anxiety and depression are real conditions and that those medications save lives." She exchanged a look with her mother. "I believe you."

As touching as the moment was, it didn't get them any closer to figuring out the events of the afternoon. He only disliked the dead man even more than before he arrived. Then he realized what Alyssa said. He hadn't known about her pills. "Are you sure he didn't know about your prescription?"

"No way," Alyssa said. "He would've berated me for being weak and discarded them."

"Mother, he would've had to care about you to go to that extreme. As long as it didn't get back to his friends, Father wouldn't have given a damn what you did with your body."

"You ungrateful brat," Alyssa snarled.

Mother and daughter spoke at once, yelling over one another. Alyssa extended long, pink nails toward her daughter, who batted her mother's hands away. They looked like they were seconds away from snatching each other bald.

"Ladies, ladies, please," Barclay implored as he tried to separate them back to their couch cushions. He had the patient demeanor of someone who'd done this more than once. "This spiteful back-and-forth isn't helping anyone, especially not the officers trying to figure out what happened with Jean Claude today."

The women stopped yelling, but they continued leaning forward to glare at one another.

Royce felt like he was on an episode of *Housewives* and wished for a bowl of popcorn. He risked a glance at Diego and bit back a laugh at the younger detective's stunned expression. Christ, they'd be talking about this case at the cop shop for a long time. "Emotions are clearly high, so let's try to get through this as quickly as possible. At the mayor's behest, we'll resume this conversation tomorrow or Monday."

The women called a truce with jerky nods before turning their attention to Royce and Diego, who moved them through the day's timeline as quickly as possible. With Barclay's mediation, they figured out that Jean Claude had been home alone for over five hours by himself, which was plenty of time for him to get worked up and search the house for ways to ease his frustration. And then there was the alcohol to consider. Alyssa admitted that she'd poured him a glass of scotch after his aggravation had reached peak levels. She'd been the one to suggest he should take a swim to relax. They didn't have security cameras anywhere on the property because they would ruin the elegant aesthetic, so there was no way of knowing when or if the doctor went for a swim or if he'd fallen into the pool during his overdose.

"How much liquor was in the decanter when you poured the drink?" Diego asked.

"It was half-full," Alyssa replied. "He'd been nursing that five-hundred-dollar bottle of scotch for six months or more."

And he drank the rest of it in one afternoon? He'd either received bad news from Richard Todd or had gotten furious when they failed to connect. Obtaining phone records would help answer that question if a judge approved a warrant in what appeared to be an open-and-shut overdose. It was possible that Mrs. Matisse had tired of his shit and slipped him the pills and plied him with the booze, but they'd need to find some evidence pointing them in that direction. The autopsy would clear things up or muddy the waters.

"How was Dr. Matisse's overall health? Did he have any underlying conditions that could've been exacerbated by the pills or alcohol?"

"No," Julia said.

"Absolutely not," Alyssa stated emphatically. "My husband was at the peak of health. He worked out religiously and adhered to strict eating habits. His only vice was an occasional glass of scotch, as I said. A single bottle would typically last him a year or longer."

She sniffed. "I gave him one for Christmas every year." She looked at her daughter. "I'm pretty sure it's the only time he liked me."

Julia's mouth trembled as she reached around the mayor to hold her mother's hands. Barclay leaned back with a wary expression on his face. "That's not true, Mother."

The last thing Royce wanted was for them to get into another argument, so he kept the conversation going. "Do any of you know the source of his distress?"

The trio averted their gazes away from him and grew pensive. Julia's brow furrowed, Alyssa glared at no one in particular, and the mayor frowned. One by one, they seemed to pull the room back into focus. The trio exchanged glances among themselves before giving Royce and Diego their attention again.

"No," they said at once.

"And I'm not sure it matters to you," Barclay added. "Unless you suspect foul play."

"Should we?" Diego asked. "Has Dr. Matisse had any issues with anyone?"

The trio looked at each other again and this time shook their heads. Barclay looked less convincing, but Royce couldn't tell if Matisse had confided in him or if he simply suspected someone with the doctor's personality had ruffled the wrong feathers. Royce wanted to push harder but knew it would likely backfire. It was time to call an end to the interview for the time being. He leaned forward and turned off the recording. He asked for one final piece of information, which was how to contact Yvonne and Ricardo.

Alyssa gave him a puzzled look. "Why? They weren't here today."

"Mother, something has been off with Father since yesterday

afternoon. Give the sergeant their contact information so he can see if they witnessed anything that might explain why this happened."

"That makes sense." Alyssa looked at Julia. "Could you get that for them? It's in my address book in my office."

"Sure," Julia said. "I'll be right back."

Silence washed over the room as they waited for her to return. Luckily, she wasn't gone long.

"You've been through a lot," Royce said, pocketing the piece of paper she gave him. "We can chat again later once you've had time to rest and assimilate everything that's happened."

Royce and Diego placed a few business cards each on the coffee table and collected their contact numbers before exiting the salon. They regrouped on the back patio where the medical examiner and her staff were loading the body bag onto the gurney.

"We better call Mendoza and bring him up to speed."

They waited until the medical examiner, crime scene techs, and officers were ready to leave and followed everyone through the house and out the front door. Royce and Diego called Mendoza from the car and gave him a rundown of what they knew so far, starting with the bomb Felix dropped on Royce. The chief said nothing until Royce and Diego finished their summary.

"Christ," Mendoza said. "This is going to turn into a media circus." He blew out a frustrated sigh. "I don't see a judge issuing subpoenas or search warrants until we get some hard facts from the medical examiner's office."

"That's what I thought too. Unless Fawkes uncovers a surprise, I can't see her ruling anything other than an overdose. And she might not be able to determine if it's accidental or not. That will lead to a lot of public speculation, but it's better than writing a report with false findings."

"True," Mendoza said. "It doesn't sound like there's anything left for you to do right now. Enjoy the rest of your night because I'll want to know how the family reacts to Felix's exposé in tomorrow's paper."

"You got it, Chief." Royce disconnected the call and looked at Diego. "Let's head on back to my house. The party should still be in full swing."

"You couldn't pay me to get into your pool again tonight," Diego said.

"I'll take that bet."

CHAPTER SIX

SAWYER RESISTED REALITY'S TUG ON THE STRINGS OF HIS consciousness with all his might, digging in the way Dolly did when she realized they were at the vet's office. Their bedroom was a calm oasis, a private island paradise in a sea of chaos that swirled around them. *Just five more minutes.* Too late. His brain was coming alive and clocking his surroundings. Beyond his closed eyelids, Sawyer could tell the sun was brighter than his typical wake time. Royce had come home from the crime scene and instigated a pool volleyball tournament that lasted until well after midnight. He'd told Sawyer that he wanted to replace the images of the Matisse swimming pool with happier ones from their house. Royce had also admitted after everyone left that he'd wanted to challenge his temporary partner's refusal to get back in the pool. Diego's resistance hadn't lasted long, and he'd ended up on the winning team. Sawyer and Royce hadn't crawled into bed until nearly two in the morning.

The sharks, their cat and dog, were circling the bed in their impatience for breakfast. Dolly's toenails clicked against the hardwood floor, and Bones' tail swished hard enough to stir the air. Sawyer kept his eyes closed to do a body scan instead of facing their outrage. He started with his feet, flexing his ankles to get the blood flowing. Then he straightened his legs, pulling his muscles taut and releasing them to feel the warmth flood those awakened areas. By the time he reached his ass, the only thing he could focus on was the press of an insistent erection between his cheeks. Sawyer tensed his glutes to pull a deep groan from Royce. He meant to scan higher to prove he could resist his husband, but Royce's delicious chuckle vibrated against Sawyer's back. A confident hand snaked around his hip, and deft fingers brushed over his hardening dick.

Royce pressed a kiss to that sensitive spot beneath his ear, and Sawyer shivered. "Want some help with your body scan?"

Sawyer pressed his ass harder against Royce's pelvis. "Yes," he whispered. "You're so thoughtful."

His husband's wicked fingers slid through the trimmed hair at the base of Sawyer's dick. Royce's chuckle sounded dark and devious. "I try." He stroked his fingers upward, circling Sawyer's belly button and making his abs flex and quiver. "Feeling awake here?"

Every cell in Sawyer's body hummed, but he swallowed hard to keep his voice even. "I think so."

"Hmmmm." Royce slowly dragged deft digits up Sawyer's taut abdomen until he reached his sternum. Then he shifted right to glide over Sawyer's pectoral muscle, circling the nipple until it hardened. Royce pinched and tugged until Sawyer cried out. "Definitely awake here."

Sawyer reached behind him and fisted his hands in Royce's hair. "Sexy fucker."

"Present," Royce said like he was answering a roll call. He slid his hand upward to cup Sawyer's jaw and turned his face to brush a kiss over his lips. "And ready."

Meow.

"Don't make eye contact," Royce whispered in his ear. "Keep those eyes closed and just feel."

Sawyer did as his husband directed and smiled when Royce reached up to retrieve the lube from the headboard caddy. The thing stored remotes, tablets, and anything else someone might use in bed to watch television or entertain themselves, which was why Royce put their lube there. He'd placed a late-night order and paid extra to get the caddy there faster when he decided separating long enough to grab the lube from the nightstand allowed too much room for Bones to pounce in the gap to wreak havoc and kill the mood. The only thing Royce guarded more fiercely than sexy time with Sawyer was his bear claw addiction. The fumbling over their heads became more frantic, and Royce released a growl born of frustration.

"Don't look it in the eye," Royce whispered in his ear as he intensified the search.

"Are you still talking about the c-a-t? Or do you mean the eager beast pressed against my ass?"

Meow.

"Of course the furry fucker can spell now," Royce growled. "Yes, I was talking about our f-e-l-i-n-e."

Meow.

"Maybe I should just get up and feed them," Sawyer said. "I can come right back to bed."

"And then we have to take Dolly for her morning walk. Real life is waiting outside our bedroom, and it will do everything it can to fuck us over while preventing us from screwing." More rustling, and Sawyer almost opened his eyes. "The lube must've slid sideways. I need a smaller pocket for it."

"Or a bigger bottle of lube," Sawyer suggested.

"I married a genius." Royce fumbled around for a few more

seconds, then cried out, "Aha!" right before a small package of snacks smacked Sawyer on the head. Royce flung the bag aside and said, "Oops. Forgot I'd tucked those in there."

Sawyer wasn't remotely surprised his husband had stashed snacks in the headboard caddy. "Sweet or salty?"

Royce nuzzled the back of Sawyer's neck and nipped at the sensitive skin there. "You're both." The *snick* of the lube cap opening signaled the end of the snack conversation and the start of filthy talk and foreplay. Before Royce coated his fingers, he slid a confident hand from the top of Sawyer's ass crack down to his lower thigh. He grabbed the back of Sawyer's leg and lifted it. "Give me what I want."

Sawyer bent his knee to expose himself to Royce's eager body. "Take it."

A cool, slick finger pressed against his puckered rim, circled a few times, and then pressed inside. Sawyer hissed in arousal as Royce teased him and hummed the tune of "Easy Like Sunday Morning."

Meow. Yip, yip, yip.

"This is a solo performance," Royce told Bones and Dolly. "Daddy doesn't need your help right now."

"Solo?" Sawyer asked. "Am I just a spectator too?"

"It's a duet. My bad."

Royce pushed two fingers inside him and continued humming and dragging slick fingers over sensitive nerve endings, making Sawyer arch his back and push his ass against Royce. "That's right. Your body is going to sing for me now."

"Damn, a trio," Sawyer whispered. "It's getting crowded in our bed."

Royce nipped his ear. "Smart-ass." Then he retracted his fingers, and Sawyer whimpered in protest. His husband's refusal to budge too far from him meant Sawyer felt the glide of a fist against his ass when Royce smeared lube on his cock. Wet fingers held Sawyer's hips in place as an eager dick pressed against his entrance. Royce slid inside him, stretching him open on a long, slick glide. Sawyer's breath hitched at the moment of penetration and exhaled in a gasp when Royce's cock nudged against his prostate.

"Ro," Sawyer whimpered with his next breath.

"I've got you, baby." Slick fingers moved from Sawyer's hips to his cock. Royce kissed the shell of his ear and nipped the lobe. "Always." Then he slowly and methodically made love to Sawyer with perfectly synchronized up-and-down strokes on his cock while lazily fucking his ass. Prostate nudges coincided with wrist twists on the head of Sawyer's dick, rendering him a bundle of frenzied need in seconds.

"Please," Sawyer begged. "Put me on my knees."

A dark chuckle rumbled from Royce's chest as he ignored Sawyer's desperate pleas. Then he simply continued to hum the song and took Sawyer apart one cell at a time with his lazy lovemaking until the pleasure was too much for either of them to withstand. Royce's thrusts and strokes sped up and lost their precision, but the wild messiness amped Sawyer up even more.

"Don't stop, baby. Please."

"Never," Royce whispered huskily. "Give it to me. Let me feel it."

Sawyer sucked in a breath as pleasure detonated inside him. He coated Royce's hand and clamped around his cock as he rode out his orgasm.

"That's it," Royce coached. "Going to fill you up." He released Sawyer's dick and rolled him onto his stomach, where he straddled Sawyer's upper thighs and spread his cheeks apart to watch his dick glide in and out of his greedy hole. "Mine."

And Sawyer basked in the glory of his husband's possession. "Yours."

Royce squeezed his ass cheeks together and pounded inside him, rutting and grinding until he came with a snarling growl that made Sawyer want to start all over again. Collapsing on top of him, Royce buried his face in Sawyer's neck. They stayed that way for several moments, lost in their private bubble as their breathing returned to normal.

Meow. Yip, yip, yip.

A furry paw smacked Sawyer in the nose, and he couldn't resist cracking open one eye. Bones stared at him with a malicious glare that promised unholy retribution if one of them didn't get out of that bed and feed him. Royce chuckled as he gingerly eased from Sawyer's ass and rose from the bed. Sawyer admired his husband's perfectly toned body as he glared at the cat and dog.

"I'm up, my little hellcat with your minion hellhound." Royce had tried for a stern voice, but he couldn't disguise the underlying layer of humor. "Are you happy now?"

Meow. Yip, yip, yip.

"Pretty sure that's a big fat no," Sawyer said.

"Or they're critiquing my performance." Royce's hand landed on Sawyer's ass with a loud *smack*. "Up and at it. Our fur kids are hungry."

Sawyer grumbled but rose from the bed. He didn't bother making it because they needed to change the sheets after the fuckfest they'd had since their clinic visit on Friday. It was Sawyer's turn to feed the beasts and start the coffee while Royce fired up the shower. Sawyer wanted to take a detour to brush his teeth, but he didn't want to incur the wrath of Bones. "I have a new title for my autobiography," Sawyer said to his majestic feline son sauntering beside him. "*Wrath of Bones. It needs a snazzy subtitle, don't you think?"

Meow. Bones wasn't the least bit impressed with the idea. He picked up his pace, expecting Sawyer to step it up too.

Yip, yip, yip. Dolly spun in excited circles at the end of the hall. He couldn't tell if she approved or was outraged on her savior's behalf.

Bones could do no wrong in her eyes ever since he'd outsmarted the house sitter and escaped to rescue the tiny, abandoned dog from the inclement weather and a life of abuse. Sawyer and Royce had returned from their honeymoon to discover Bones had adopted a tiny dog, and it hadn't taken them long to fall in love with her too.

"Doll Doll agrees with me." Sawyer hummed as he considered. "Something like, *How an Ordinary Man Became His Feline's Bitch.*"

Dolly barked her approval, and Bones threw him a disgusted look over his shoulder. Sawyer noticed the extra swagger in Bones' steps and swish in his tail though.

He made quick work of feeding the beasts and starting the coffee. They typically used the single-serve option throughout the week, filling their mugs on their way out the door. Sundays were made to savor the joys in life—big and small. He grabbed the Kona coffee Kelsey had brought them back from Hawaii. She'd taken a long vacation with Andrew and Ella before committing her body to producing and carrying their baby for nine months. Sawyer lifted the bag of grounds to his nose and inhaled the aroma. "If heaven had a smell…" Sawyer took one more big sniff before adding grounds to the filter, checking the water level, and starting the machine. He jogged through the house in his haste to enjoy his husband naked and wet, a phenomenon he'd never tire of.

Royce looked up when he burst into the bathroom, and his lips curved into a sexy smirk when Sawyer didn't bother to hide his admiration. He turned to face Sawyer, propping his forearms above his head on the glass doors. "Like what you see?"

Sawyer stood rooted in place and raked his gaze over Royce's sheer perfection. "You know I do. I can't ever get enough of you." Which was why Sawyer found it comical when Royce felt threatened by another man.

Royce arched a brow. "Then what are you waiting for?"

The invitation snapped Sawyer from his haze. He went to the sink to brush his teeth and wash his face. Royce opened the door for him as he approached the shower. Sawyer stepped inside the enclosure and got lost in wet kisses and soapy caresses until the drop in the water temperature signaled the heater had reached its capacity.

"We're going to invest in a tankless water heater someday," Royce grumbled as he aggressively toweled his hair.

"I think that defeats the purpose of us trying to conserve water by showering together," Sawyer said.

Royce dragged the towel from his head and stared at his husband in disbelief. "You do know that no one means it when they say that."

"I know a bullshit excuse when I hear one," Sawyer quipped. "But it wouldn't hurt us to turn the faucet off between the soaping and rinsing or the sucking and the fucking."

Royce stepped off the shower mat and stalked toward him, not stopping until he had Sawyer pressed against the vanity. "Fine, but you're taking the brunt of the cold-water blast when we turn the faucet back on. You shouldn't mind the chill since you keep threatening to install a tub on the patio for cold water plunging." Royce, who preferred a hot tub even in the dead of a sultry summer, shivered at the mere thought.

Sawyer cupped his face. "Cold water is good for you. It helps with inflammation."

Royce kissed him hard on the mouth. "I'll take your word for it."

They finished drying off and got dressed to take Dolly for her morning walk. She waited by the door where they kept her harness and leash. Sawyer sighed and shook his head when he saw that the gear hanging from the designated hook matched the Americana bow in her hair. The groomers recognized a sucker when Royce sauntered through their doors with a five-pound dog tucked under his impressive biceps. Sawyer didn't remark on Dolly's latest ensemble, but Royce knew him well.

"She likes it," Royce said as he hooked the leash into the loop on her harness. "Don't you, baby girl?"

Yip, yip, yip. Dolly spun in enthusiastic circles to punctuate her response.

"See! She likes it," Royce said.

"She has to pee," Sawyer countered as he snatched the poop bag dispenser from its hook.

"Probably that too."

Dolly got a walk every day, come hell or high water, but she especially loved to lollygag on Sundays. Royce claimed their dog possessed an internal calendar to go with the clock that told her when it was time to eat. Sawyer had claimed it was because she fed off their energy. Either way, she was content to sniff the flowers planted in the beds at the ends of their neighbors' driveways and investigate every tree and swath of grass until she found the perfect place to squat.

"You didn't tell me what you learned at Dr. Matisse's house last night," Sawyer said.

"There's not much to say right now." Royce launched into a summary of what he'd seen and the conversations he'd had at the doctor's house. Sawyer tried to focus on what Royce said, but his thoughts drifted to things he didn't want to explore.

The pep talk they'd had before Royce left the previous night didn't fully quell the growing unease in the pit of his stomach. Sawyer and Royce were excellent judges of character, but they got things wrong too. Look at the way they'd misjudged one another when they first met. Even if Dr. Flores was as wonderful and as capable as they believed her to be, honest mistakes occurred every day. What if the technicians accidentally mislabeled something or handed the wrong sperm sample to the doctor for insemination? Honest mistakes were just as painful as intentional ones. They wouldn't know if the baby biologically belonged to them without testing. And if she didn't? Was the universe telling him that he wasn't meant to be a father?

Royce's hand settled on the nape of his neck and gently squeezed. "Knock it off."

Sawyer inhaled deeply and pulled himself together. "I don't know what you're talking about."

Royce halted in the middle of the sidewalk, forcing Sawyer to stop too. "You're freaking out again."

"Was not."

"Yes, you were." Royce kissed him, and the tension eased. No matter what happened, they'd tackle it together. "I was telling you about the dynamics between the Matisse women, and you didn't acknowledge it."

Sawyer chuckled, and they resumed walking. "Intense?"

"It was *Housewives* material," Royce replied. "There was so much tension between mother and daughter."

"Do you think that's significant?" Sawyer asked.

"Not sure, but I felt bad for Julia. I just got the feeling that she was always striving for her father's approval, and Mayor Barclay confirmed it."

"And now she'll never get it," Sawyer said.

"Exactly." He halted suddenly and pointed at the Sunday paper lying in the middle of a neighbor's yard. "I forgot all about Felix's exposé. Do you think he went ahead with publishing it?"

Sawyer snorted. "Do you wake each morning with an erection?"

Royce whistled for Dolly, and they stepped up the pace to encourage her to poop. Because they wanted her to, the dog took her good ole time finding the right blades of grass to bless. Sawyer waited with a bag at the ready and swooped in once they accomplished their feat. They had a digital subscription to the paper, so Royce brought his tablet into the kitchen and pulled up the article on it.

"Do you mind if I read this? I'm sure Felix only gave us a CliffsNotes version of the dirt they'd dug up on Dr. Matisse."

"Read it out loud," Sawyer said. "I'll wash up and start breakfast."

"Do you want me to attempt a foreign accent to make this more entertaining?" Royce asked. "I won't be nearly as good as your favorite audiobook narrators."

Sawyer laughed. "Just read it."

While he diced vegetables for egg white omelets, Royce read an accounting of horrific behavior spanning forty years. He sucked in a breath and then cursed.

"What?" Sawyer asked.

"Felix claims the doctor fathered nearly five hundred children in forty years and points out that there could be hundreds more who've never taken DNA tests."

Sawyer nearly sliced off a finger with that staggering revelation. He set the knife on the counter and faced Royce. "Almost five hundred? He told us about forty-eight."

"Those were just the ones he'd traced to the doctor's Savannah practice. There are four hundred and eighty-two confirmed matches as of now," Royce said. "That breaks down to twelve children a year. What's the likelihood he kept to one fraudulent insemination a month?"

Sawyer leaned back against the counter. "It's not likely at all. I'm not an expert in psychiatry, but there is surely a term for someone like him. Narcissist doesn't sound severe enough for someone who willfully procreated with unsuspecting women. He was a damn predator. Was he trying to create a super race of people like him?" Sawyer's fears from earlier rushed to the forefront of his mind, but he shoved them aside before they could drag him down like a dangerous undertow lurking beneath the surface. "What else does the article say?"

"The number of victims is really the only thing Felix didn't touch on last night. I'm sure there will be more to come in the podcast and follow-up segments for the paper." Royce set the tablet down and scrubbed a hand over his face. "Christ, what a mess."

"I can't imagine what his wife or daughter must be feeling. Surely someone in their inner circle has read the article this morning and told them about it." Sawyer met Royce's gray eyes across the kitchen. "If neither of them killed him, they're going to wish they had."

Royce's phone rang before he could respond. He looked at the device and said, "It's the commissioner. Top brass on a Sunday morning is never a good thing." He tapped a button on the phone before greeting Commissioner Rigby. "I'd bet a thousand dollars you aren't calling to get Sawyer's recipe for strawberry and cream scones."

A dry laugh crackled through the phone's speakers. "You should've bet ten thousand," she replied. "Though the recipe sounds delicious. Are you at home?"

"Yes, ma'am. I have you on speakerphone, but it's just Sawyer and me."

"Morning, ma'am," Sawyer said.

Rigby greeted him warmly before getting down to business. "I've received a phone call from both the mayor and the Matisses' family friend, a retired lawyer named Richard Todd. Alyssa and Julia Matisse are aware of accusations stated in Felix Franklin's article. They are understandably in shock and in denial. Richard Todd has asked that you hold off on speaking with them further until they've had some time to process another devastating blow. He's asked for a meeting at nine on Tuesday morning at their home."

"What did Mayor Barclay say?" Royce asked.

"He mostly repeated what Richard Todd had already requested, but I could tell he was on a fishing expedition to see what we knew about Dr. Matisse's death."

Royce snorted. "Of course he was. What did you tell them?"

"Based on the information I received from Mendoza last night, I didn't see a reason to push the issue today," Rigby said. "I agreed to honor their wishes unless we received concerning updates from the medical examiner."

"I agree with you," Royce told her. "Fawkes told me it might be a few days before she has preliminary reports to share."

"I wouldn't count on that," Rigby said. "The mayor is adamant there won't be signs of foul play, and Richard Todd wants to shelter his friends from undue speculation and suspicion. Both had planned to call Dr. Fawkes after speaking to me to apply pressure. I wouldn't leave town if I were you."

"Now I feel like a suspect," Royce teased.

"Sorry," Rigby said. "I didn't mean to sound so ominous. My gut just tells me the Matisse death won't be as cut-and-dry as Todd and Barclay hope."

Sawyer had the same feeling of foreboding, but that probably had more to do with the personal fears this case triggered.

"Don't worry about me, ma'am." Royce's steely gray eyes never wavered from Sawyer's face. "I'm going to enjoy the rest of the holiday weekend with my family and not give this case another thought until someone gives me a reason to." Royce might've said those words in response to Rigby's comment, but Sawyer knew he was the intended target.

"Good to hear. I'll keep you posted if I hear anything new, and I ask that you do the same."

"Yes, ma'am."

Royce disconnected the call and set the phone on the table. He stood up and crossed the room to stand in front of Sawyer. "I meant what I said. We're not letting this son of a bitch ruin our dreams or even taint our weekend. Maybe I get called in, and maybe I don't. I sure as hell will not waste precious time by worrying about something that hasn't happened yet." He kissed Sawyer hard on the mouth and then moved to the pantry. "You make the omelets, and I'm going to whip up a special treat."

Sawyer watched his husband remove ingredients from the pantry and set them on the counter. He tried to guess the surprise from the items and had landed on pancakes until Royce placed a bottle of white vinegar on the counter. "What in the world are you up to, Ro?"

"Buttermilk pancakes. Aunt Tipsy taught me how to make them."

"We don't have buttermilk," Sawyer replied.

"That's what the vinegar is for. You can make your own by adding it to regular milk."

Sawyer arched a brow. "Come on."

"Wait and see."

Thirty-five minutes later, Sawyer pushed back from the table and held up his hands in surrender. "I will never doubt you again."

Royce wiped a smear of syrup from his face with his napkin, but his smug smile remained. "What are your plans this morning?"

"I need to make some side dishes to take to my parents this afternoon, but I can hold off on that for a while."

Royce waggled his brows. "Oh yeah?"

He couldn't mean another round of sex. Had Royce discovered the fountain of youth while he'd been in Denver? "I'm all yours."

Royce's mouth spread into a wicked smile that would make the Joker jealous. "That's what I'm talking about. I'll grab the keys."

"Keys?" Sawyer repeated.

"The hardware store is having a Memorial Day weekend sale."

Sawyer groaned and hung his head in defeat. "But you already have one of everything from there."

Royce pushed back his chair and stood up. "I could use some extra muscle carrying out the potting soil." He stopped by Sawyer's chair long enough to drop a kiss on the back of his neck.

Sawyer pushed back from the table with his empty plate in his hand and followed Royce to the sink. "Fine." The lack of enthusiasm in his voice made his husband laugh.

"And we could look at paint color samples. I'm thinking something neutral, like the palest gray, yellow, or green."

Sawyer didn't have to ask what room Royce wanted to paint. "You don't want to wait until we're certain?"

"I'm going all in," Royce said. "What do you say?"

All the turmoil Sawyer had felt vanished as he stared into his husband's mercurial eyes. "I'm quite partial to the color gray for a nursery color."

"Grab the keys and let's go."

CHAPTER SEVEN

ROYCE RUBBED HIS HANDS TOGETHER IN GLEE WHEN SAWYER parked in his parents' driveway. "I should've worn sweats."

Sawyer shook his head as he turned off the car. "It's not Thanksgiving."

"If Evangeline hosts a food gathering, it will be a feast worthy of stretchy waistbands."

"You remind me of Joey from *Friends* when it comes to food," Sawyer teased.

Royce waggled his brows and grinned. "How you doin'?"

"Your New York accent could use some work."

Royce accepted the challenge as he climbed from the passenger seat. He opened the back door, and Dolly enthusiastically wagged her tail in her doggie car seat. "How you doin'?" Royce asked her.

Yip, yip, yip.

"That one was a little better," Sawyer called from the rear of the car.

Royce unsnapped Dolly's three-point harness system that kept her securely in place. The memory of their doggie car seat search made him smile. Sawyer had been determined to find the highest-quality product with the best safety rating, and Royce insisted on one that also looked cute enough for their princess. He figured the purchase had created the blueprint for thousands of future parenthood negotiations. Some would take days to decide, like the doggie car seat, and others would click into place immediately, such as the pale gray paint they'd found for the nursery. Their only debate at the hardware store had been how many gallons to buy. The nursery wouldn't be a large space, but Royce knew the one-coat promise from most paint brands was complete bull-shit. And then there was the primer to consider. Did they prep the walls first or buy a paint with the primer built in? Sawyer left that decision up to him, and Royce had gone with the combo option for expediency since they weren't trying to cover a dark paint color.

Royce lifted their dog from the ultra-safe and super-snazzy seat and cradled her to his chest. "Dolly loved my accent. Isn't that right, sweetheart?"

"She also licks her ass," Sawyer reminded Royce right as the dog swiped her tongue against his cheek.

"Oh man." Royce wiped Dolly's saliva off his face and vowed to do a thorough wash as soon as they passed off their food offerings and the granddog to Evangeline.

Sawyer leaned against the car and laughed. "We couldn't have timed that any better."

"We? Only two out of the three Stooges were in on the gag, Asshole." Royce tried to sound irritated, but that only made Sawyer laugh harder.

A car pulled up behind them, and they both turned to see who'd arrived. Royce didn't recognize the silver sedan, but he knew the man Sawyer referred to as the silver fox behind the wheel. He was used to seeing his father drive a Harley or a pickup truck with enough horse-power to prove his masculinity. Had Eddie gone out and purchased something as prosaic as a sedan? And was that a relaxed smile on his face as he looked toward the passenger seat? A joyous grin? Royce failed to name the expression because he'd never seen it on his father's face before. Then a weird thing happened. Royce felt his own mouth curve upward at the corners. *No, no, no.* He didn't smile when seeing Eddie or observing him. *Abort grin. Abort grin.* But his lips still kept stretching until they reached their limits.

"Well, well, well. This must be the new friend he mentioned at graduation night," Sawyer said.

Royce shifted his attention to the passenger seat, where a woman with auburn hair smiled at Eddie like he'd hung the moon. The unexpected joy he felt moments ago turned to dread in the pit of his stomach. *Oh damn.* It never ended well for anyone who loved Eddie Locke. "New friend?" Royce asked.

"Oh damn," Sawyer replied. "I forgot to tell you that part. Eddie asked Evangeline if he could bring a new friend."

Royce turned an incredulous look on him. "You forgot to tell me?" When Sawyer just shrugged, he added, "Don't get attached."

Sawyer cut him a look that implored Royce to play nice. He could be very, very nice, and his husband damn well knew it, but they could get in their car and go home if Sawyer needed a reminder. There were still so many things he wanted to do with his husband to make up for lost time. His thoughts must've bled into his expression because Sawyer's pleading eyes heated with anticipation until he blinked and pulled himself together. "Nice try, Asshole."

"I don't know what you're talking about." Royce widened his eyes innocently, but it only made Sawyer scowl.

"We're not going home, so tuck your rizz away for later."

Royce groaned. "Oh no, you didn't just say that."

Sawyer's wide-eyed innocence looked much more believable when he aimed it at Royce. "What? I was just speaking your language."

"It's not *my* language," Royce countered. "It's what the youths say, and I was looking forward to a break from their awful dialogue." He hadn't repeated half the weird shit they said because it would annoy the Ivy League right out of Sawyer.

"Well, rizz definitely applies to the Lockes. Charisma oozes out of your pores with the pheromones."

Royce grabbed the collar of his shirt and tugged it away from his neck. "More like sweat. It's going to be a hot one."

"Sweat. So cringe." When Royce only glared at him, Sawyer leaned forward and kissed his frowning mouth. "Relax. Breathe. Give your dad a chance."

Car doors shut, and Dolly wriggled excitedly when she saw Eddie. Royce watched his father and the mystery lady approach them. "How many chances are too many?" Royce whispered.

"Royce," Eddie said before Sawyer could respond. He extended his large, calloused hand toward his son, forcing Royce to reciprocate or look like a jerk.

He forced a pleasant smile on his face as he clasped his dad's hand and gave it a firm pump. "Eddie, it's good to see you."

It took Royce a second to realize he'd meant it. He felt a softening in his chest and bit back a silent curse. Apparently, another chance wasn't too many. Royce had to tighten his hold on Dolly, who was doing her best to leap into Eddie's arms. She'd get her chance because his dad was a real sucker for the tiny dog, but Eddie was too busy grinning fondly at Sawyer and shaking his hand.

"Settle down, sweetheart," Royce whispered to the dog before kissing the top of her head. "Grandpa is demonstrating good manners. You could take a lesson from him."

"That's the first time someone accused me of modeling good behavior," Eddie joked.

Royce chuckled. "Credit where credit's due."

Dolly yipped her frustration at being ignored, and Eddie gave her his full attention. He held out his hands toward her, and the little dog's body vibrated with excitement. Royce laughed as he carefully transferred the dog to his dad. Royce would never forget the day Eddie met Dolly. He'd expected his dad to make shitty remarks about him having such a sissy dog, but Eddie had fallen hard and fast for the Yorkie.

"How's my best girl?" Eddie asked as he lifted her up for a kiss. This interaction, Royce knew, was a hundred percent genuine.

"Hey," the auburn-haired woman chided. "I thought I was your best girl." She pursed her glossy pink lips into a cute pout. Up close, this woman was a stunner. She'd applied her makeup like a pro, drawing focus to her finest features, like pale green eyes, high cheekbones, and full lips. Her lightly tanned skin was flawless except for a smattering of freckles across her nose and the barest hint of lines at the corners of her eyes and bracketing her mouth.

Eddie held up a finger to his lips and tipped his head toward the dog, who watched him with unabashed adoration. Dolly wormed against his chest like she was trying to burrow herself inside him, and her tongue licked the air because she couldn't reach his face. "She'll hear you." Then he ducked his head down and let Dolly kiss his cheek.

Royce was just about to warn Eddie that the dog had most likely licked her ass at some point that day, but a light-hearted laugh caught Royce's full attention. Eddie's friend was tall and willowy, the antithesis of Eddie's usual type. He typically went for women who were short and curvy with bawdy laughs. The playful sounds coming from the lady who watched Eddie with heart eyes were infectious. She wore a sage-green sleeveless dress with scalloped edges ending just above her knees. Her sandals were the wedged kind and made from that material that looked like frayed rope. He couldn't remember what it was called but knew they were popular and often expensive. Kelsey didn't find it funny when Royce offered to make her the same pair of shoes for less money. He'd even shown her the different rope options he had in his garage, but no go.

"I think she likes you," the woman said as she lifted her hand to pet Dolly.

The little dog tensed, flattened her ears, and narrowed her eyes at the interloper reaching for her. Royce's eyes widened, and his lips moved to yell "noooooooooooooo." Sawyer's arms appeared in Royce's periphery as he reached for the dog. But neither of them was quick enough. Their little darling Dolly turned into the Yorkshire Terror right in front of their eyes. Her warning bark was high-pitched and terrifying. Eddie's new friend snatched her hand back and giggled nervously, but that wasn't enough to please the six pounds of pissed-off fur. One corner of Dolly's mouth curled up, and she growled viciously, her tiny body vibrating with jealousy.

"Oh my." The lady held up her hands in peace and backed away a few steps. "My bad."

"She doesn't mean any harm," Eddie told her, though Royce wasn't sure how his lips could form words with that wide, cocky grin taking up so much real estate on his face.

"I'm so sorry," Royce said, extending his hand. "Our dog is just a bit possessive about Eddie, which is really irritating."

Eddie's smug grin faded into a scowl. "Because I'm not worthy of her devotion?" His dad's voice was gruffer than usual, and he sounded highly insulted. He no longer looked like the carefree man who'd arrived just minutes ago.

Royce reacted the way he always did at the first sign of conflict with Eddie. He tensed from head to toe and went straight into fight mode. "No," Royce replied tersely.

Sawyer's hand landed at the small of his back, a gesture Eddie's dark gray eyes didn't miss. Would his father recognize the act as love and comfort, or would he view it as Sawyer trying to tame him like a wild animal? Maybe both things were true at the same time. Eddie knew how to raise Royce's hackles better than anyone on the planet, but Sawyer's soothing touch reminded him that neither he nor his father were the men they used to be.

Royce forced his shoulders down and softened the tension in his face. "I just meant that we're doing all the work, and she loves you the most."

The good-natured smile returned to Eddie's face. "That's just the perks that come with grandparenthood. I'm just the good-time guy who gets to show her all the love without having to train or discipline her. Isn't that right, Doll Doll?" The dog yipped her agreement and licked Eddie's cheek.

"The same phenomenon happens with my grandcat." The woman smiled at Royce and extended her hand. "Hello, I'm Jolene, but my friends just call me Jo." She rolled her eyes. "Or they sing certain lyrics to me."

"Royce," he said, shaking her hand. "No wonder Dolly doesn't like you."

Jolene giggled and winked at the outraged dog. "I'm not looking to take your man."

"Forgive my sh—um—crappy manners." Eddie's stammered apology was awkward and oddly endearing. "Royce is my second-oldest son."

"The problematic middle child," Royce teased.

Eddie scoffed and shook his head. "Don't listen to him. He's been a great kid, always looking out for everyone he cares about. I'm not at all surprised he became a cop."

Royce glanced over at Sawyer. He had to be dreaming, right?

Sawyer's features formed a brief "I told you so" expression before he turned his attention to Jo.

"Oh, and this is Royce's husband, Sawyer," Eddie said. "Jo is the new friend I told you about."

Royce shot his husband another disbelieving look as he introduced himself to Dolly's nemesis. Then he looked at his father with objective eyes. Eddie's polo shirt was different than the one he'd worn to the graduation ceremony. Were they buy-one-get-one-free purchases? Did Eddie have a closet full of preppy clothes now? His jeans didn't have a single hole in them, and the brown leather belt at his waist didn't feature a wallet chain or metal ornamentation. Royce was oddly comforted by the familiar leather biker boots on Eddie's feet. He understood his father was trying to become a better version of himself, but he didn't want the man to become unrecognizable. And was this a change Eddie wanted or one he thought he needed? One *Jolene* thought Eddie needed?

"You've got smoke coming from your ears, kid," Eddie said. "Don't overthink it."

"That's my fault," Sawyer said. "He picked up that bad habit from me."

Eddie clapped Sawyer on the shoulder and looked at Jo. "My son-in-law doesn't have bad habits. The world would be a better place if more people were like him."

Jo grinned at both Royce and Sawyer. "Just so you know, he's said that about both of you more than once."

Eddie grimaced, then asked, "Do I repeat myself obnoxiously?"

Jo shook her head. "You're a proud father. I think it's wonderful."

"I'm trying to be the father my kids deserve." Eddie might've responded to Jo's comment, but his steely gaze was locked on Royce, as if willing him to believe the words. "It's long overdue."

And Royce wanted to trust him. Sawyer had faith in Eddie's intentions, and that should've been enough for Royce. His husband had exceptional intuition, but then again, he'd never really witnessed Eddie during his darkest hours. Royce struggled to see anything else when he looked at his father. He sometimes woke in the middle of the night after nightmares of becoming another Eddie. Royce and his dad had taken positive steps forward, only to shuffle backward more times than he wanted to count. Could this time be different? The expression in Eddie's eyes said it was, and he'd sure dressed the part and brought the right accessories. Royce immediately scratched that thought. It was cruel and disrespectful to a lovely woman who didn't deserve it. He was sick to his stomach that the thought had even crossed his mind.

Royce wanted to blame Eddie's past influence, but this was all him, and he mentally apologized to a person who thankfully couldn't read his thoughts. Royce dreaded telling Sawyer the path his thoughts had taken, but he would. He told his husband everything—the good, the bad, and the freaking ugly. Sawyer was his salvation, the shiny beacon of what good people could be, and Royce really wanted to be good people. He'd surrounded himself with the finest humans on the planet since meeting Sawyer Key, hoping their decency would rub off on him. Why couldn't he allow himself to believe Eddie wanted the same? Couldn't Jolene be his shiny beacon of hope? Why the hell did he sound like the sappiest dickhead to live? Because he was, and he loved the person he'd become. Just maybe Eddie saw something in Royce that made him think he could do it too. *Cue the moody classical music. Someone just had a breakthrough.* Snarky quips aside, a weight had been lifted off Royce's shoulders with the epiphany, which was why he decided to extend an olive branch to Eddie. Well, maybe not a branch. Perhaps a fragile twig that would snap easily, but it was a start.

Royce turned to Sawyer. "Why don't you show Jo around and

introduce her to everyone? I already know Evangeline will adore her. Eddie, Dolly, and I will take the food inside." *And find a private place to talk.*

His father looked at Jo, and the couple exchanged so much with that single glance. It reminded Royce of the life he'd built with Sawyer. He turned and met warm, chocolate-brown eyes. Quicker than he could blink, Royce had expressed how hard he was trying, and Sawyer let him see his unabashed pride at Royce's effort. A snarly growl interrupted the sweet moment when Jo tried to emphasize her support with a pat on Eddie's shoulder.

"I'll win you over, Dolly," Jo vowed. "Just you wait and see."

Sawyer approached Jo and extended his elbow. She looped her arm through his with a gracious smile. "This is how you treat people, Doll Doll. Notice I didn't try to bite off a finger."

"Dolly is pure Locke," Eddie said. "It's going to take a long time to retrain her bad habits."

Sawyer and Jo laughed as they strode away, but Eddie wasn't wrong. It was the entire reason Royce hadn't wanted to submit his sperm for consideration.

Eddie peered into the trunk of Sawyer's car with a raised brow. "Should I have brought something too?" He sounded unsure and embarrassed. That small display of vulnerability drew Royce closer to his father than any of Eddie's previous past displays of toxic masculinity. "I asked Evangeline, but she told me not to worry about it. I really struggle to read social cues. Was that really a code for yes? Kind of like when a woman—er—partner tells you everything is fine when it's definitely not?"

Royce chuckled and clapped Eddie's shoulder. Dolly curled her lip as if to snarl, but Royce quelled her behavior with a single glare. "Evangeline is a straight shooter, Eddie. If she told you not to bring something, then she meant it. The Keys always make more food than necessary."

Eddie gestured to the trunk. "Then what's all this?"

Royce sighed, shook his head, and hoisted a massive tote with at least three types of Southern salads in there and one hoity-toity, super-healthy kind that probably only Sawyer would eat. "This is just my husband."

Eddie shrugged and reached inside the trunk with his free hand to hoist an equally large bag holding desserts. "You lead," he said.

Royce led him around the side of the house to the backyard, where the party was already in full swing. People chatted, sipped colorful beverages, and engaged in games on the expansive lawn stretching to the river. Royce turned to check Eddie's reaction and was surprised to see an easy smile on his face. He followed his father's gaze and smiled when Evangeline greeted Jo with a hug upon introduction. Royce nudged Eddie to get his attention and nodded toward the house. "Come on, Romeo."

Eddie fell in step beside him and said, "I'm not a literary expert, but I'm almost positive *Romeo and Juliet* isn't a love story."

"It's a tragedy," Royce said.

"I want the love story." Eddie halted suddenly, and Royce stopped too. "I want to be the kind of man Jo deserves." He swallowed hard, and the color leached from his tan face. "To be the kind of man your mama deserved but didn't get."

Royce had talked to his father enough over the past few years to know Eddie deeply regretted many things about his life, and the way he treated the mother of his children topped the list. Believing Eddie wanted to change and trusting him to carry it out were two very different things. For the first time in decades, Royce believed Eddie might be capable of both aims. "I want that for you too, Eddie." He continued to walk toward the house. "Jolene seems like a really nice lady."

Dolly growled as deeply as a tiny dog could, and Eddie shushed her. Royce was pretty sure he heard his dad land a playful kiss on top of Dolly's head.

"These bows," Eddie said. "Does she have one for every holiday?"

"And season. I have a problem," Royce admitted. "And that groomer recognizes a sucker when we waltz into her salon."

"I'm sure she can use the support in this economy," Eddie said. "It's got to be rough owning a small business in this day and age. Between the DIY videos on YouTube and same-day delivery from Amazon, everyone thinks they're an expert on everything, and they expect the tools to fuck shit up to arrive within hours."

Royce nearly tripped over his feet when he stepped through the open atrium doors at the back of the house. He figured the price of gas and beer was the extent of Eddie's economic knowledge, but his father had surprised him with thoughtful commentary. Royce had the sudden urge to explore Eddie's opinion on other topics, but it wasn't the time or place. There was one pressing thing he had to know, so after they dropped off the food in the kitchen, Royce led Eddie to a small sitting room that overlooked the backyard. Sawyer and Jo were still talking to Evangeline and Barron. Eddie watched their interactions for a beat too long because Dolly growled at him.

"Don't be sassy," Eddie gently scolded as he sat in a club chair that faced away from the windows.

"Pretty sure she was born that way," Royce replied as he took a seat opposite his dad. "How'd you meet Jo?"

Eddie held his gaze long enough for the pause to feel awkward. Royce was a thousand percent sure he hadn't picked her up at one of his local haunts. "I met her at a PFLAG meeting."

"A PFLAG meeting?" Royce repeated.

"Yeah, that's what I said." There wasn't a hint of annoyance in Eddie's voice. He sounded nervous instead. "It's an organization for parents and allies of—"

"I know what PFLAG is, Eddie. I'm surprised to learn that you do. When did you become involved with the organization?"

Eddie puffed up his cheeks and huffed out an exhale while rubbing the back of his neck. "I went to my first meeting about five months ago. It was after our last argument."

"The one where you disrespected my husband in his own home?" Royce hadn't meant to raise his voice, but it occurred naturally when speaking to his father.

To his credit, Eddie remained calm and stroked his big hand over Dolly's tiny back. Royce couldn't tell if Eddie was comforting himself or the dog. "I didn't mean to disrespect Sawyer—in his home or otherwise. You know I like him a lot. And I meant what I said earlier. The world would be a better place if we were all like Sawyer. I am sorry about what I said. I never meant to sound disapproving about you having kids with him. I think you'd make a wonderful dad. I just thought you didn't want to have children."

"That was true until I met Sawyer. Kids were always going to be a part of his future. I needed to get on board or let the train pull out of the station without me." Royce thought back to the earlier days in his relationship with Sawyer when everything was so new and scary. He hadn't known how they'd arrived at love or where they'd go next, but Royce had wanted Sawyer and would've done anything to make their relationship work. That meant a lot of healing and growing in ways that made Royce extremely uncomfortable at the time, but all the hard work became the tracks he laid so he could chug his way toward a beautiful life. "Eddie, you didn't just express surprise that I wanted kids. You questioned why I hadn't chosen an easier path since I'm bisexual. That's the part where you disrespected my husband. There's a lot of shit I'll tolerate, Eddie, but never that. And it makes me question if you've ever truly known what love is."

His father winced at the memory. "Does he know I said something so stupid?"

"No," Royce said. "And I didn't withhold the details of our argument to protect you."

"Then why?"

Royce let his gaze wander out the window, where children squealed with delight as they chased one another on the lawn. He'd never thought about why he'd kept Eddie's latest gaffe to himself. Sure, it would've hurt Sawyer's feelings, but he would've worked through it like healthy adults do. He would've said that Eddie only asked a question most people would've been afraid to, and he would've reached the point where he commended Eddie's curiosity and viewed it as a step in the right direction. Royce could even picture Sawyer saying something like "learning is growing." No, he hadn't kept quiet to protect Sawyer. So why? The truth hit Royce hard and stole his breath as he met Eddie's anxious gray eyes. They both realized this was a big step in their relationship. "I kept it to myself to protect you, to keep this moment right here a possibility. I saw the acknowledgment in your gaze when I pointed out how wrong you were to suggest such a thing. You weren't ready to admit your mistake out loud, but I thought there might come a moment when you would. And maybe I didn't want to make it harder on you to apologize and put things right."

Eddie scrubbed a hand over his face and exhaled heavily. "I don't deserve your forgiveness, but I want it." He paused to swallow hard before continuing. "I was wrong to say what I did. There's no way I'd want you to turn your back on the guy you love just to choose an easier path. Hell, I can't imagine you with anyone else. Sawyer is it for you. I'm truly sorry for what I said."

"Thank you, Eddie," Royce said. "And I accept your apology."

Eddie expelled a long breath. "And I learned I don't have to understand every damn thing to accept it."

Royce arched a brow. "Wow. That's awfully woke of you, Eddie. I'm impressed."

His father snorted. "Well, they were running a sale at the store. Buy a polo shirt and get some empathy and compassion for free." He looked down at his chest and pulled the shirt fabric from his body. "Do I look stupid?" He raised his chin and met Royce's gaze head-on, letting him see genuine vulnerability. "Or do I look like an actor trying to portray a decent guy?"

Royce scoffed. "You look very handsome. Sawyer calls you a silver fox."

"Clearly, the man has good taste," Eddie said, gesturing between the two of them.

"But you don't have to change your clothes to be a different person on the inside," Royce told him. "If this is what you want to wear, then strut your stuff. But if you don't think Jo will like you if—"

"This wasn't her idea," Eddie said. "I just wanted to try something new." He looked down at himself again briefly. "I like how I feel when I wear nicer clothes."

"That's all that matters," Royce said. "Tell me about PFLAG and Jo."

"I'd told a lesbian on my construction crew about our argument. She let me have it with both barrels and told me about PFLAG. It took me a few weeks to work up my courage to attend a meeting, but I went. I felt foolish and so out of place, but the people went out of their way to make me feel comfortable. It took a couple of weeks before I let my guard down long enough to have an honest conversation with the group. It helped to talk to parents of bisexual sons in same-sex relationships."

"It also didn't hurt that one of the parents was exceptionally pretty," Royce teased.

Eddie chuckled, and a pink blush crept up his neck. "I was already on the right path when Jo arrived on the scene. Her daughter had just come out as pansexual, and Jo wanted to take all the right steps to support her." Eddie inhaled deeply and pressed two fingers to his sternum.

"Are you experiencing chest pains?"

Eddie nodded but held up his hand when Royce reached for his phone to call 911. "Not those kinds of pains. The growing kind, I think." He swallowed hard and kissed the top of Dolly's head. The little dog licked his cheek excitedly. "Jo scares me." He shook his head. "No, that's not right. Damn, all this talking about shit is hard." His honesty made Royce smile, but he didn't risk saying anything that would ruin the moment. "My feelings for Jo scare me." Eddie continued to rub his sternum. "I haven't felt this way about a woman since I met your mama. My track record with good women is downright terrible. I'm afraid to love Jo almost as much as I am to lose her."

Royce pinched his forearm to see if he was dreaming. The gesture caught Eddie's attention, and he snorted. So much for not ruining the moment.

"Smart-ass," Eddie said.

"I come by it naturally."

"That's for damn sure." Eddie ran a hand through his hair. "I'm a damn mess, aren't I?"

Royce smiled at his dad. "That's how you know you've found a good one. Giving in to the fear is easy, but you'll regret it for the rest of your life. Putting yourself out there is risky, but the rewards are worth it. And if you don't think you deserve her, then do the work until you do." Moments of his life with Sawyer flashed through his mind like a beautiful slideshow. He relived the moment they got engaged and exchanged vows. He replayed grocery store shenanigans and backyard barbecues. Royce thought about the trip to the fertility clinic and the myriad ways they'd celebrated their love, like slow sex on Sundays. Hot damn, risking his battered heart and putting in the effort to become a better man was so worth it.

Eddie stared at him for several moments before he nodded. "You're right." He slapped his knees and stood up. "You're wearing that dopey expression you get every time you think about Sawyer."

"Guilty, but maybe I'm more like you than I realize." When Eddie only tilted his head, Royce continued. "You should see your face when you look at Jo."

The blush from earlier turned a darker shade of pink on his father's skin. "She's incredible. And not just her looks," Eddie quickly added. "She's intelligent and thoughtful. I don't think Jo knows a stranger, and she always has something kind to say. And the way she parents… is incredible." Eddie lowered his head to look at Dolly. He lifted the small dog up and softened his voice. "That's how moms and dads are supposed to be, Doll Doll. They're not supposed to make their kids afraid to be themselves."

A tingling sensation began in Royce's nose, and tears stung the back of his eyes. He blinked before they could form because Eddie hadn't reached that level of openness yet, but he sure appreciated the steps his dad had already taken.

Eddie lifted his head once more and met Royce's gaze. "That's the kind of parent you'll be."

Emotion clogged his throat, and Royce swallowed hard so he could respond. "I hope so, Eddie."

"I know you will. I, uh, I'm proud of you, Royce. You've made a wonderful life for yourself with your career and your husband. You really impressed me at the graduation ceremony on Thursday. Those kids are lucky to have you as an influence."

"Thank you for being there. It meant a lot to me."

Eddie scrubbed a hand over his face again before he said, "Getting deep in here, isn't it?"

Royce could tell his dad wanted to pull himself together. "Sure is." He rose to his feet and reached for Dolly. "I'll take her so you can get within a foot of Jo."

"Appreciate it."

Dolly gave him a little sass when he tried to take her from Eddie, but her tantrum didn't last long, and she offered an apology by licking his cheek. Royce pulled a leash from his back pocket and connected it to her harness. He usually let her run free at the Keys' house, but there were too many people at the barbecue. Royce didn't want her tripping anyone, and he surely didn't want her to get trampled. Dolly's distaste for Jo was another concern to consider. "Sorry," Royce told her. "Just for today."

They retraced their steps into the backyard and joined Sawyer and Jo in conversation with Evangeline and Barron. After they exchanged pleasantries, Eddie struck up a conversation with Barron about his new smoker. The next thing Royce knew, their fathers were exchanging tips and recipes like lifelong friends. Eddie moved with an ease Royce had never seen before, and he decided to stop questioning the change and enjoy it.

Sometime later, after stuffing their faces with an exorbitant amount of food and playing more lawn games than Royce dreamed possible, Sawyer pressed his lips to Royce's ear. "Told you so."

They'd snuck off to the dock to enjoy a few private minutes alone.

He'd planned to tell Sawyer all about the conversation he'd had with Eddie until his husband got smug with him. "You did," Royce said instead. "Right as always."

"I caught bits and pieces of conversations about Dr. Matisse today."

"It's shaping up to be quite a scandal."

"Sure, but these chats sounded more personal," Sawyer said. "I bet there are a lot of people here who know him."

Royce didn't doubt that Barron and Evangeline ran in a similar circle to the doctor's family. "There's nothing to investigate until something or someone gives me a reason to."

As if he'd tickled the mighty cosmos' taint, Royce's cell phone rang.

CHAPTER EIGHT

"IT'S THE MEDICAL EXAMINER'S OFFICE," ROYCE SAID. AND SINCE he only had one active case, he was pretty sure Dr. Fawkes was about to give him the something or someone he needed to investigate.

Sawyer shook his head in resignation. "You just had to tempt fate."

"Sorry," Royce said before answering the call. "Why do I have the feeling you're about to blow up my holiday weekend, Doc?"

"Because I am," she said dryly. "And maybe it's only fair since I've hardly left the building since we delivered Dr. Matisse to the morgue. Something about misery loving company, perhaps?"

"Would you like me to bring you something good to eat?" Royce had learned long ago that the staff at the medical examiner's office had iron stomachs. Nothing put them off their food.

"My husband already delivered a care package, but thank you for offering," Fawkes said before getting down to business. "There are two sets of fingerprints on the poolside pill bottle, but neither belongs to Dr. Matisse. We ran the prints through IAFIS but didn't get a hit."

Royce's spine straightened so fast he felt something crack in his lower back. "I bet I know who they belong to."

"Perhaps. One set is also on the liquor decanter and the tumbler, along with Dr. Matisse's."

"The matching set will belong to Alyssa Matisse. The prescription belonged to her, and she told us she'd poured her husband a drink to settle his nerves."

"That is a logical deduction, but you'll need to get a warrant to obtain her fingerprints. Based on the phone calls I've received from Chief Mendoza, Commissioner Rigby, Mayor Barclay, and someone named Richard Todd, it seems the widow doesn't plan to participate in the investigation." Dr. Fawkes' droll tone made it clear how she felt about the constant intrusions and the roadblock.

"I'll also get a warrant for Julia Matisse's prints as well, though the third set on the pill bottle could belong to someone working in the pharmacy. What else did you find?"

"There wasn't enough benzodiazepine in his system to kill Dr. Fawkes on its own, but his alcohol level was more than twice the legal limit. Oh, and the drugs weren't ingested whole," Dr. Fawkes said. "They were ground up and added to a green beverage. I'd say a smoothie, based on the large amount of blended spinach, kale, banana, and protein he ingested. I can confirm that there was no residue from the pills in the tumbler or decanter, only traces of the alcohol."

"Someone ground up the benzos and put them in his smoothie." Wife or daughter? That was the question. Dr. Matisse had hundreds of angry victims, and some of them might've been out for blood, but it was unlikely they'd gotten past security without inside help. Royce made a mental note to check if the security team had documented deliveries to the Matisse house on Saturday morning or afternoon. That was a tried-and-true method murderers use because people still fell for it. "What is Matisse's official cause of death?"

"The combination of alcohol and benzodiazepine triggered

respiratory and cardiac failure. His autopsy also revealed pulmonary and cerebral edemas, which are both pretty standard finds with drug overdoses. By my calculations, Dr. Matisse had been dead for a minimum of three hours before his daughter found him in the pool. Because he hadn't administered the pills himself, my preliminary report will list his death as suspicious. That should help you obtain the necessary warrants."

"Thanks for getting back to me so soon," Royce said. "I'm sorry you're missing out on spending time with your family."

"It's par for the course. We both knew what we would sacrifice in this line of work," Fawkes said. "I gave the bulk of my staff time off for the holiday, so I only have a skeleton crew assisting me. No pun intended," she added before Royce could comment. "So, I likely won't have additional information for a few more days."

"What you've provided will grant my warrants if I can find a judge who doesn't care about the doctor's connections."

"Judge Stanley," Fawkes said. "She's a straight shooter and doesn't give a damn about where you came from or who your daddy is. She cares about justice, honesty, and integrity." The medical examiner snorted. "I sound like her campaign manager now. Sorry about that."

"No apology necessary. Judge Stanley it is."

Viola Stanley had made quite an impression after her recent election, but Royce hadn't crossed paths with her yet. He made a mental note to change that. Royce and Tara welcomed guest speakers from every corner of the justice system. The county prosecutor and the public defender's office participated each year, so why not bring in a judge and maybe do a mock trial? Most police officers had to testify in courtrooms at some point in their careers, so it would be a good experience. "I appreciate you, Dr. Fawkes. Talk soon."

After they disconnected, Royce called Diego. The younger

detective answered with a growl before complaining that he hadn't gotten to eat the hand-churned ice cream and his favorite cake yet.

"What's your favorite cake?" Royce couldn't help but ask.

"Yellow with chocolate icing."

"You're such a basic bitch, Fuentes."

"Don't forget hungry as hell," Diego said.

Levi's laughter drifted through the speaker. "Dee, you've eaten enough food for five people. I'll make sure no one eats all the cake and ice cream."

"I'll do you one better," Royce said. "I'll write up the warrants and submit them for signature. You enjoy your cake and get ready to look menacing."

"Warrants? Whoa! What happened?"

Royce filled him in on what he'd learned from Dr. Fawkes. "It should be enough to get fingerprints from Alyssa and Julia."

"Wow, okay," Diego said. "I'll be ready for your call."

After they disconnected, Royce turned to his husband. "Sorry. Again."

Sawyer shook his head as he stood up. He extended his hand and assisted Royce to his feet. "I'm ready to leave anyway. Let's grab Dolly, say our goodbyes, and head out. You'll need to change clothes before you go."

They made their way down the dock and over the lawn until they reached Eddie, who watched their approach with an unreadable expression. He wasn't sure how he was going to say goodbye to his dad until he stood in front of him. Royce opened his arms and hugged Eddie, who stiffened in surprise before returning the embrace and squeezing his son tight. They separated and gave each other matching back slaps to ease any awkwardness.

"I'd like for you both to come to our house for dinner," Royce said. "Maybe next weekend?"

"Yeah," Eddie said. "That sounds great." He looked at Jo for her reaction.

"I'd be delighted." She hugged both Royce and Sawyer without a single yip out of Dolly until Jo wrapped her arm around Eddie's waist. The dog issued a warning growl that made the grown-ups laugh.

"I'll call you in a few days, Eddie. We'll hammer out the details, and I'll invite the rest of your heathens to meet Jo." Except for the one serving time after trying to kill Sawyer. Royce would happily let that little fucker rot behind bars.

Eddie nodded, his eyes looking suspiciously moist. "All of them at once?" He looked at Jo again to gauge her reaction.

"Bring it on," she said.

Dolly yipped and barked ferociously and nearly leaped from Sawyer's arms.

Royce stroked the silky fur on top of her head. "She wasn't challenging you, little miss. We better get this hellion out of here before it gets ugly."

"Be careful," Eddie told Royce. "Cruelty and evil taints every zip code."

Royce hadn't told his father what case he was working on, but it wouldn't have been hard for him to figure it out after the news broke. "I will."

"You made your dad cry," Sawyer whispered after Eddie and Jo were no longer in earshot.

"I have that effect on people," Royce teased.

Sawyer nudged him but didn't comment further.

"Why haven't you asked about my conversation with Eddie?" Royce asked.

"You'll tell me when you're ready."

And he would as soon as he believed he hadn't dreamed the entire thing.

Royce didn't have to ask if Diego had eaten his cake because there was a smudge of chocolate icing at the corner of his mouth. He should've told the younger detective right away, but he kept the tidbit to himself during the trip to the Oaks, through the brief interview at the security booth, and for the drive up to the Matisses' home. Getting the warrants signed had been easier and faster than Royce had predicted, but the sun had started to set by the time he turned into the long driveway. The dense trees blocked the remaining daylight, making the surrounding forest look dark and dangerous. An eerie vibe settled over the SUV as they made the last turn toward the mansion.

Maybe it was because Royce suspected one of the Matisse women killed Jean Claude. Finding out that there was no record of visitors or deliveries the previous day strengthened his resolve. The only other two who could've had easy access to Matisse or his food had left the previous day and hadn't returned, according to the security guard's records. Royce would contact both the housekeeper and the chef to take official statements about what they witnessed in the house on Friday, but not until after he spoke with Alyssa and Julia. He couldn't risk the women destroying evidence if they caught wind that the investigation into Dr. Matisse's death had swung in a different direction.

"Maybe the women worked together to kill him," Diego said.

"The thought crossed my mind, especially if either of them overheard Dr. Matisse's conversations with Felix or Richard Todd."

Royce parked behind a silver Mercedes and got out of the vehicle.

He gestured for the CSU van to pull up next to him, forming a little blockade. His search warrant was limited in scope, so only two techs climbed from the van and approached them. Hattie March and Shannon Juarez looked young enough to be in Royce's Explorer Academy, but he wasn't stupid enough to say that out loud. Besides, he'd worked with them long enough to know they were older than they appeared.

Hattie, a shy Black woman, squinted up at Diego while Royce read through the warrant and told them what he needed them to look for. When he finished talking, Hattie got Diego's attention and gestured at her own mouth with her index finger. "You got a little something…"

Diego whipped out his cell phone and checked out his appearance in the camera's selfie setting. He rubbed the icing smear off his face and then glared at Royce. "Were you going to tell me I had chocolate on my face?"

Royce forced his eyes wide. "Is that what that was? I thought it was a Madonna beauty mark."

Shannon, an outgoing Latina, scrunched up her nose and looked at her partner. "Who?"

"Children," Royce huffed in frustration.

"Don't listen to Grandpa," Diego told them. "It's past his bedtime."

The massive double doors opened before Royce could respond. Mayor Barclay and a silver-haired man Royce presumed was Richard Todd strode onto the massive front porch.

"Detectives, this behavior is completely inappropriate," the silver-haired man said. "I'm Richard Todd, the family's spokesperson. I talked to Commissioner Rigby this morning and stressed that the Matisses didn't wish to be bothered after Jean Claude's sudden death and the ghastly slander the local paper printed this morning. The commissioner assured her cooperation. I'm going to call her and—"

Royce silenced him by holding up documents even a first-year law student would recognize. "Commissioner Rigby knows I'm here. I spoke with her before I filed for my warrant."

"Warrant?" Richard asked. "On what basis?"

Royce handed the legal document to the man before addressing the mayor, who had remained surprisingly calm. "Commissioner Rigby agreed to delay our meeting unless we received information from the medical examiner that prompted a more urgent conversation. We wouldn't be here otherwise."

"I understand," Mayor Barclay said, though he didn't sound happy about it.

Richard sputtered as he read through the documents. "I don't believe this." The warrant didn't summarize their suspicions, but it provided the scope of their search and seizure, which often betrayed the direction of their investigation. It was a delicate dance between legal transparency and keeping the cards close to the vest until it was time to reveal your hand. In Royce's favor, he didn't think either Alyssa or Julia were seasoned criminals who'd made an art form out of getting away with murder. Richard turned to Barclay and said, "The police think Julia or Alyssa killed Jean Claude."

Mayor Barclay furrowed his brow. "That's impossible."

"Not in my line of work, sir," Royce said. "And we're not accusing Julia or Alyssa of anything. We're gathering additional evidence for the investigation into Dr. Matisse's death. The process could also exonerate your clients."

"Try that bullshit on someone who hasn't practiced law for nearly four decades," Richard scoffed as he smacked the warrant against the mayor's chest. "I might be retired, but I'm not stupid."

Barclay flinched before taking the paperwork from his hand. "I'm not a lawyer, Rick. I don't know what I'm reading."

Richard opened his mouth to answer him, but Royce held up a hand. "I want to have this conversation just once. Step aside so Detective Fuentes and I can come in with our technicians. I'll need to speak with Alyssa and Julia Matisse immediately."

"Do as he says, Rick," Mayor Barclay said. "I know Commissioner Rigby well. They wouldn't be here without just cause."

"It's utter bullshit." The attorney's face was a startling shade of red as he glared at Royce.

"We'll have to let this play out because neither you nor I can disregard a warrant. I don't know about you, but I have no intention of going to jail for obstructing justice."

It didn't seem like Richard Todd intended to cooperate, but after a prolonged silent exchange between the men, the attorney stepped aside and gestured for them to enter. His dark eyes flashed with outrage, and he jabbed his finger in the air near Royce. "I intend to watch you closely and ensure you don't search or seize anything not specifically spelled out in this warrant."

"That won't be a problem, sir." Royce might've sounded like a calm professional, but he really wanted to snap the pretentious man's finger off and shove it up his ass.

Royce led the team into the kitchen. The CSU techs had already donned protective gear upon entering the residence to prevent evidence contamination. Royce and Diego pulled on gloves, too, as a precaution. "We're looking for anything that could've been used to grind pills into a fine powder," Royce said. "A mortar and pestle, or maybe a coffee or spice grinder. The warrant names both manual and electronic options. We're also looking for any equipment used to make and consume smoothies. I suggest starting in the dishwasher. Collecting indoor and outdoor trash is also included in the warrant."

Julia and Alyssa rushed into the room. They both looked

disheveled, as if the commotion of unexpected people and noises had dragged them from serene solitude. Julia had one towel wound around her head and another wrapped around her body. "What the fuck is going on?"

Alyssa's hair was sticking up at odd angles, and she rubbed sleepily at her eyes. She hadn't dressed for bed but must've fallen asleep. The weary widow looked at Richard Todd. "Is it Tuesday already?" That must've been some nap.

"Christ, Mom," Julia hissed. "It's Sunday evening. The detectives didn't honor the bargain their commissioner agreed to."

Mayor Barclay moved to stand in front of her. He lifted his hands as if to settle them on her shoulders but then dropped them to his side when considering her state of undress. "Julia," he cautioned. "The medical examiner returned some troubling information that won't allow delay."

Julia brushed the mayor aside and approached the lawyer, who seemed unwilling to look in her direction. "Uncle Rick, fix this."

The silver-haired man sighed and turned his rigid body around to address her. "Dear, this situation is outside my scope of expertise, even if I was still practicing. I told your father that on Friday, and I'm telling you now."

Julia's pale face turned a mottled red. "Don't say another word about your conversations with my father."

"Julia," Alyssa said sleepily. "What are you wearing?"

"Excuse me, Mother. I was in the bathtub trying to forget about the horrors of the past few days."

That remark caught Royce's attention. Her father had only been dead for a little over a day. Sure, Julia could've misspoken, but her previous conversation about Dr. Matisse's behavior implied that tensions had been high since her arrival. Or had she known about the allegations?

Had Julia's daddy issues gotten the best of her when she learned Dr. Matisse had potentially fathered hundreds of other children? Did it magnify her anger toward him enough to kill?

"That's no excuse for such unladylike behavior," Alyssa said. "Eli and Richard are extremely uncomfortable, and you're making a horrible impression with these detectives and…" Her voice trailed off as she waved at the technicians searching her kitchen for evidence. Alyssa seemed too calm under the circumstances. Had she been able to refill her prescription, or was she completely unaware of the seriousness of the situation? She'd aimed her only outward display of ire at her daughter.

"Drop it, Mother," Julia snapped. "We have bigger fish to fry. The police must think one of us killed Father."

"Go get dressed," Alyssa insisted. "Now."

Julia glared at her mother, and Royce couldn't help but imagine what her teen years had been like. After a tense standoff, Julia spun on her heels and flounced out of the room.

Alyssa smoothed a finger over her eyebrows and then used her hands to tidy her hair. "I'd offer everyone a beverage, but you've seized control of my kitchen."

"We won't be long, ma'am," Diego said.

"Why are you here?" Alyssa asked.

"Let's wait until your daughter returns," Royce said. "That way, I only have to say this once."

"Efficient," Alyssa said with an approving nod.

A few minutes later, Julia returned to the kitchen looking much younger than her thirty-eight years in a pair of faded skinny jeans and a coral tank top. Then again, her mother didn't look seventy-five either. Had Alyssa intentionally waited until her late thirties to have a child, or were her fertility struggles what prompted Dr. Matisse to specialize in the field?

"This is barely an improvement over the towel," Alyssa said when she noticed Julia's outfit.

"Shut it, Mother." Julia turned a scathing expression on Royce and Diego. "Why are you here, and what are you looking for?"

Royce wasn't one to tip his hand, but he couldn't shake the impression that one of these women, or possibly both, had acted rashly when they put the ground benzos into the green smoothie and served a scotch chaser. Their emotions might've gotten the best of them, and they hadn't likely covered their trail very well. He glanced over his shoulder and noticed that the techs had already bagged and tagged several pieces of evidence from the dishwasher, including a single-serving blender cup and a dirty glass—both with a dried green residue clinging to the sides. They'd also found what looked like a collection container from an electric spice grinder. When he turned back to face the Matisse women, he noticed their attention was riveted to the activities behind him. Richard Todd and Mayor Barclay were regarding one another in what looked like a silent conversation. "Dr. Matisse ingested a deadly combination of alcohol and benzodiazepine, resulting in respiratory and cardiac failure."

Four sets of eyes jerked to him. Their reactions were what he expected since everyone had jumped to this conclusion the previous day based on the empty decanter of liquor and the bottle of pills on the poolside table. No one seemed surprised, but only the men looked irritated. As for Julia and Alyssa, their faces had become masks of indifference that made it impossible to know what they were thinking. Royce was pretty sure that would change soon because it was unlikely their lessons on becoming a genteel lady included how to react when someone accused them of murder, not that he planned to do so right then. A mere hint of suspicion should do the trick nicely.

Richard Todd was the first to verbalize his thoughts. "That's the ruling we expected the medical examiner to find. So why the warrant to seize certain household items and collect fingerprints?"

"Fingerprints?" Alyssa asked. "Whose?"

"Yours and your daughters," Diego replied.

Alyssa placed her hand on her chest as if to clutch her pearls, but she wasn't wearing jewelry. "Why would you need our fingerprints?"

Diego discreetly nodded his head in deference to Royce, signaling for him to take the lead.

After letting the question hang in the air for an uncomfortable silent stretch, Royce squared his shoulders and focused his full attention on the Matisse women. "Because Dr. Matisse's fingerprints were nowhere on the pill bottle found by the pool. He didn't ingest whole pills. He consumed benzodiazepines that had been ground into a fine powder and mixed into a smoothie. There were two other sets of prints on the prescription bottle, and we need to know who had handled it."

His dramatics paid off when their neutral masks briefly slipped to expose their genuine reactions. Alyssa's mouth dropped open in shock, and she turned her head to look at her daughter, which meant she caught the devastation that temporarily twisted Julia's features. Mother and daughter met one another's gaze, and something flashed between them, but it was gone in the next second. Royce had to give it to them though. Both Julia and Alyssa quickly popped those cool, unreadable masks back into place. The entire range of emotions lasted mere seconds, and if he hadn't been watching them closely, he would've missed their reactions entirely. Had they acted together? It was something he couldn't ignore.

"You need better legal advice than I can offer," Richard said. "I told

Jean Claude the same thing when he called me on Friday afternoon to tell me about the impending exposé."

"I told you to stop talking," Julia snarled.

"I'm not breaking privilege because I wasn't acting as your father's attorney on Friday, and I'm not acting as yours now. I'm a retired estate attorney, Julia. The best I can do for you now is to give you the name of a criminal attorney."

Julia snorted. "As if I trust your recommendations."

"Stop acting like a spoiled brat, Julia," Alyssa said. "There has to be an explanation that doesn't include murder. There's no way to get around the warrant?" She'd aimed her question at Richard, who shook his head. "Fine. Let's give them our fingerprints. The quicker these people get what they need, the faster they'll leave."

"What time did you speak to Dr. Matisse on Friday?" Royce asked the lawyer.

"It was around noon," Richard replied. "I returned his call during my lunch break."

"Do you know if Dr. Matisse was at home at the time of the call?"

"To the best of my knowledge, he was," Richard said.

"Stop offering information," Julia said.

"I'm not obstructing this investigation," Richard Todd told her. "Even if my conversation with your father fell within the scope of client-attorney privilege, the time and location it occurred isn't privileged information."

"Fine," Julia said. "I refuse to answer questions without legal representation present. And since Richard has clearly and repeatedly stated that he can't advise us properly, any conversation you wish to have with us will have to wait until we can find an attorney who can." She held out her hands in front of them. "Print us and get out."

Royce shrugged and reached for the fingerprinting field kit the

CSU team had set on the island for him. "The evidence will talk loud enough for everyone," he said.

Julia went first. Defiance stiffened her resolve and her fingers, making it harder to roll her prints onto the card. She snatched the alcohol packet he handed her once he finished.

"You aren't under arrest, Ms. Matisse, but I need to ask you not to leave the area until we've solved the investigation."

"Fuck off," Julia snarled before storming from the room.

Alyssa stood quietly and watched her daughter's dramatic exit before sighing and willfully complying with the process. "I'm sorry about Julia's outbursts," she said. "This entire ordeal is extremely upsetting." Her bottom lip trembled, and Richard swept in to place a comforting arm around her shoulders. "Finding Jean Claude in the pool the way she did, and now these dastardly character assassinations…"

"I'm not offended, Mrs. Matisse," he assured her. "And I am terribly sorry to add to the duress your family is suffering. We'll be out of here soon."

Alyssa nodded weakly. "I think I'll just go back to my room." She turned to Richard. "Do you mind supervising all of this?"

"It's not a problem. Elliott and I will clean up after they leave. You won't even know they were ever here."

"Thank you," she sighed.

Richard pulled her into a tight hug, and Royce saw a telling expression wash over his features before he clawed it back. Richard Todd was in love with Alyssa Matisse. Did she return his feelings? It was hard to say just from looking at her expression and body language. Richard met his gaze and slowly pulled back from the embrace. "Go on up."

Alyssa nodded again and moved toward the hallway, but Royce called out to stop her. She looked over her shoulder and said, "I won't leave town either."

Left with just the men, one angry and the other quietly contempla-tive, Royce and Diego joined in the search and seizure. They didn't want to be there any longer than necessary, and it had nothing to do with it being a holiday weekend. The house was cold, sterile, and downright hostile at times. They could keep their money and misery, and Royce would go home to the warm and amazing life he'd built with Sawyer.

CHAPTER NINE

SAWYER FLOPPED ONTO THE SOFA ON MONDAY MORNING AND noted the way his pets watched him with pitying expressions. "What? I'm entering my Moping Era," he told them. "And that's capital *M* and capital *E*, in case you're wondering."

Dolly and Bones looked at one another, and he would've sworn a silent communication passed between them. What were they saying about him? He growled in frustration over his own ridiculousness. Dolly and Bones weren't human, even though he treated them as such. Sawyer needed to stop projecting his anxious, self-pitying thoughts onto his pets because they couldn't think and reason like he did. But that didn't stop him from talking to them like they understood his struggles.

"Yeah, I'm a mess." He'd tried to hide his melancholy by pretending to be asleep when Royce kissed him before leaving. But the ruse hadn't worked, and Royce nuzzled his nose in Sawyer's neck before kissing a path up to his ear.

"Call Kelsey and do something fun today," he'd whispered. "Keep your mind busy so you don't ruminate on the past or work yourself up over things that haven't happened yet."

"You think you know me?" Sawyer had asked groggily.

A soft chuckle had rumbled from Royce's chest. The sound was warm and tender, and Sawyer had wanted to wrap it around him like a blanket cocoon. "I know you better than I know myself. I love you."

"Love you too."

Royce had placed one last kiss on his cheek before leaving their bedroom. Sawyer had tried to go back to sleep, but his husband's predictions had been spot-on, so he'd thrown back the covers and dove into his usual morning routine for himself and the pets. Then he started cleaning their already spotless house while listening to podcast episodes on healing anxiety and working through trauma responses. The combination of movement and positive encouragement helped get him into a good headspace, but an undercurrent of angst still rippled beneath his skin and made him itchy. As long as Sawyer kept moving, he could ignore the sensation. He debated doing a deeper clean, like moving appliances to scrub under and behind them, when his phone chimed with a notification. He picked it up and saw a Ring camera alert for activity in front of the house. His pulse raced with excitement at the prospect of Royce returning home, but a ball of warmth formed in his chest when he played the video and saw Kelsey's vehicle pull into the driveway instead.

He leaped from the couch and jogged to the front door, yanking it open as she stepped onto the porch wearing a strapless yellow romper that was almost as sunny as her smile. She'd pulled her curls into a ponytail and wore a white-and-yellow-patterned headscarf. Kels had accessorized the look with chunky asymmetrical earrings and a collection of white and yellow bangle bracelets on her wrists. She was barefaced and as fresh as the tiny daisies dotting the thin yellow straps of her flip-flops. She'd slung her purse and an oversized tote over one shoulder and carried a paper bag with handles in the other.

Sawyer released a slow whistle. "You look like you just walked off the set of *Palm Royale*." They'd loved the costumes from the first season and Ricky Martin, of course. The guy just kept getting sexier with age. "Have you ever looked less than gorgeous for a single day of your life?" Sawyer asked. "And don't you dare mention childbirth because I've seen the pictures, and you looked like a million bucks after pushing a human out of your body."

Kelsey snorted and rolled her eyes, but her smile grew impossibly bigger. "I took a few minutes to tidy up before I let Andrew take pictures of me holding Ella. I was a hot-ass mess."

"Huh-uh," Sawyer said dismissively. He'd visited Kelsey at the hospital when she was in active labor. A sheen of sweat had coated her face as she breathed through an intense contraction. Maybe she considered herself a hot mess, but Sawyer had never seen anyone look more fiercely beautiful. A hard lump lodged in his throat when he realized that he and Royce would get to share this experience with Kelsey when she brought their baby into the world. Not if, when. He had to believe and not let negative thoughts win. Sawyer tried to say more, but the words wouldn't come.

"I know." Kelsey lowered the paper bag to the porch and wrapped her arms around him.

Sawyer held her as close as the bulky tote permitted and breathed in her comforting jasmine-and-vanilla scent. A deep breath dislodged the lump, freeing his vocal cords. "I'm so grateful for you."

Kelsey pulled back and patted his cheek. "And that's before you know about the goodies I brought for us." She picked up the paper bag and turned it so he could see the bakery logo on it.

"Good thing my shorts have an elastic waistband." He relieved Kelsey of her burdens and stepped aside so she could enter. "Did Royce ask you to check on me?" Sawyer asked as he shut the door and followed

Kelsey to the kitchen. He doubted very much that her appearance was serendipitous after the comment Royce had made before leaving.

"No." Kelsey set her purse on an island stool and then turned to face him. "I texted him to see how he was holding up while investigating the Matisse case."

"And that's when he told you I was moping around and creating problems that haven't happened yet?"

Kelsey shook her head. "He expressed the mindfuck this situation was having on every person who'd ever visited a fertility clinic." She reached for Sawyer's hand and squeezed. "You should call Dr. Flores and talk to her about the situation. She can give you assurances that will ease your anxieties."

"She's going to get bombarded with calls. Every person who has sought her services will freak out."

"Understandably so," Kelsey said. "But it is her job to reassure her patients that they aren't a victim of a heinous crime."

"I'll consider it," Sawyer told her. "Are you okay?" They'd talked numerous times since the news broke, but Kelsey's resolve was as unflappable as her faith in Dr. Flores.

"I am because I won't entertain the idea that some random dude's sperm could've been blasted into my uterus, either intentionally or by accident."

Sawyer cringed at the images her words created. "That's an unimaginable violation that should have serious repercussions. Fraud just doesn't seem like a harsh enough classification."

"Matisse wasn't the only doctor to pull this shit. Fertility procedures were so new when he started that there weren't many laws and regulations governing the treatments." Kelsey sighed. "Unfortunately, I don't think we've moved the needle forward much since then. All the attention focuses on the financial fraud aspect and not the emotional trauma of what feels like the deepest betrayal to these victims." She inhaled deeply and shook her body on the exhale, as if to physically purge the bad thoughts. "I'm here to distract you and not feed into your fears." She held out her hand for her tote bag, and Sawyer passed it to her. Kelsey pulled out a large tablet and grinned. "Royce told me you picked out a color for the baby's room. How do you feel about creating a Pinterest board for decorating ideas?"

It felt like something he should do with Royce, though his husband showed more interest in the high-tech gadgets like the electric baby swing with a wide base that gently and quietly swayed from side to side. Picking out the paint color had all been for Sawyer's benefit. Hesitation must've shown in his face because Kelsey placed a cool hand on his arm.

"Or not. I don't mean to overstep," she said.

Sawyer was quick to assure her. "You're not. We don't have a clue about what babies need, and we welcome your input." He gestured to her abdomen and added, "There won't be a baby without you, so…"

Kelsey stepped forward and cupped his face with both hands. "Sweetheart, I volunteered to help create and carry a baby for you and Royce. There's nothing more I want to do than help you both realize your dreams of growing your family. That said, being your surrogate slash best friend doesn't entitle me to make decisions about the baby's nursery, how they'll dress, or where they'll go to school."

Sawyer grimaced. "That sounds harsh."

"It's honest, and I need to remind myself of the role I've chosen." She cocked her head to the side and smiled. "I'm going to have opinions."

"You? I'm shocked," Sawyer teased.

"Mm-hmm. But that doesn't mean I need to air them." Kelsey briefly placed a finger over his mouth before he could respond. "Your friendship means the world to me, and I think it's important we acknowledge this arrangement might get hard at times. I can't grow a human inside my body without forming an emotional bond, no matter how many times I tell myself that he or she won't be mine to keep. You and Royce will have your own set of fears to battle, even though you both trust me with your whole hearts. Utmost honesty is going to be crucial here, and we might need to establish boundaries to preserve relationships we all value as much as our marriages. But all the challenges will all be worth it in the end because the baby will have the most amazing dads and the most stylish auntie on the planet."

"Our child will have the most stylish *godmother*," Sawyer corrected. "And he or she will know what an amazing gift you've given us. Every birthday and milestone will happen because of your selflessness."

Kelsey hugged, shook her head, and then patted her head. "Fine. You can erect a statue of me in the new backyard that Royce is probably sketching in his head after his trip to Dr. Matisse's house."

Sawyer snorted. "He told you about the gardens too? I've lost track of how many times he's mentioned the layout and the goddess water fountain."

Kelsey struck a dramatic pose and said, "I'm not a goddess, but my husband thinks I am. Does that count?"

"Absolutely."

He leaned over the bag from the French bakery and peered inside. The smell of buttery, flaky pastry made his mouth water. "Croissants?"

"Four different varieties." Kelsey pulled several containers from her tote bag and set them onto the counter. "And I brought all the ingredients to make Greek yogurt parfaits."

"French pastries and Greek dairy products," Sawyer said.

"I say we go to our favorite Mexican restaurant for a late lunch or early dinner and score an international eating trifecta."

"You have the best ideas," Sawyer said. "Which is why I'd love to build a Pinterest board for the baby with you. I'll show it to Royce, and we'll add or delete things as we go. Thank you, Kels. I really need this—*us*—today."

"I did too." She pecked a quick kiss to his cheek before retrieving bowls from the cabinet. "I brought tropical fruits, strawberries, and blueberries. The smallest container has the homemade granola Andrew makes. It tastes so much better than anything you can buy in the store, and it's much better for you."

Sawyer pulled the box of croissants from the bag and lifted it to his nose. "Nothing unhealthy about the amount of butter I'm about to consume in one of these."

Kelsey laughed as she began spooning vanilla yogurt into a bowl. "We both know it's all about balance."

Sawyer opened the box and bit back a moan. "I think Royce has rubbed off on me."

That earned a snort from his friend. "Pretty sure he does that multiple times a week, love."

Grinning, Sawyer met Kelsie's knowing grin. "I was referring to my newfound obsession with pastries. But yeah, the other thing is also very true." He waggled his brows. "Twice on Sundays."

She slapped his shoulder and snagged the box of croissants from his hand. "Attaboy."

Sawyer had always been open with Kelsey, never shying away from any subject, including things Royce might not be enthusiastic about her knowing. But that's how best friends rolled. Kelsey talked freely about her physical relationship with Andrew, so he knew they were just as amorous as Sawyer and Royce. The thought made him pause. In all the planning for the baby, he'd never considered how the pregnancy might interfere with Kelsey and Andrew's sex life. It felt a little late to bring it up, but he'd ruminate and make himself miserable if he didn't. And Kels had said honesty was crucial. "Um, Kels, is the pregnancy going to interfere with your love life? I know Andrew finds you incredibly sexy when pregnant, but will it be an issue physically?"

"Not unless there are unforeseeable complications." Kelsey pointed at him. "Don't go borrowing trouble. There's no reason to believe anything will go awry. If this pregnancy is like my last one…" A wicked grin spread across her face. "Andrew will need to double up on vitamins and get plenty of protein because pregnancy hormones make ya girl crazy horny. My man had the best sex of our lives when I was pregnant with Ella. Why do you think he jumped all over the surrogacy idea when I brought it up to him? He's going to reap all the benefits without having to care for a newborn."

"But there's the long recovery afterward when you won't be able to have sex," Sawyer said.

"Baby, that's when my man will get to recover too." She leaned closer and lowered her voice, even though there was no one to overhear them except for the cat and dog. "And we both know there are other ways to please our men."

Their shared laughter eased Sawyer's tension, and he kissed her cheek. "You're the best."

Kelsey placed a hand on her chest. "That's what I keep telling people, but I swear you're the only one who gets it."

They laughed and talked about random things as they built parfaits and picked their croissants. Sawyer went with a honey lavender, and Kelsey chose the decadent chocolate.

"Do you want to sit out by the pool?" Sawyer asked.

"Hell yes. I brought my swimsuit so I can soak up the sun and float lazily in the pool."

"You're welcome to enjoy it anytime. You could've brought Andrew and Ella too."

She held a finger to her lips. "Shhh. Mama needed a little break with her bestie."

"I'm so glad you're here."

Sawyer poured orange juice for Kelsey and made another cup of coffee for himself. They talked about random things while they enjoyed the treats Kelsey brought. Eventually, their conversation veered to work as it often did.

"What was your impression of Alec Bishop?" Kelsey asked. "I'm not sure what to make of him."

"Contrary to what Royce claims, I spent very little time around him. I think the side of his personality he shows to the public might differ from what he displays privately. He's more introspective during his speaking engagement and comes across as almost shy. He was much more outgoing and relaxed one-on-one."

Kelsey's shoulders straightened, and she tilted her head. "That's interesting. The two of you had just met, so why did he let his hair down with you?"

"Royce thinks he wants to fuck me."

Kelsey's dark brow shot up. "Does he?"

Shrugging, Sawyer said, "I don't know."

"Which of his personas is the real one?"

Sawyer sat back in his chair and pondered her question. "Honestly, they both feel genuine."

"Maybe he has a personality disorder, or he's a Gemini like you," Kelsey teased.

"Nice, Kels. Thanks."

"But seriously, there's no denying Alec Bishop did a good thing.

A *great* thing," she amended. "Exposing his father's evil actions at the cost of his own freedom and anonymity is commendable."

"Very," Sawyer agreed.

Kelsey ran her finger along the rim of her juice glass as she considered him. "But you're not convinced."

Shrugging, Sawyer said, "I'm a skeptic by nature, and I've always questioned things." He took the last sip of coffee. "Especially something that's too good to be true."

"Or someone."

Sawyer tipped his head to acknowledge her remark. "And Alec only wanted to talk about potential unsolved cases instead of the ones authorities already closed. He's fixated on finding new victims and bringing their stories to light. That's where I started to suspect that Alec is more enamored with the limelight than getting justice or providing closure."

"How so?" Kelsey asked.

"Nothing he has done so far focuses on the victims or includes their families. His best-selling book details his life with Andrew and the moment he uncovered the cache of evidence that suggested his father could be a serial killer. He briefly named each identified victim, but we don't learn anything about them. It's almost like an editor said, 'Hey, it feels like a real dick move not to acknowledge your father's victims,' and so Alec did, but without giving any color to their lives. They've stayed one-dimensional, grayscale background characters in the narrative, while Andrew and Alec are these vibrant, dimensional characters. Why would I expect him to treat new victims any different?" Sawyer realized his face was hot, and his pulse was faster. He took a deep breath and exhaled. "I didn't realize how much that bothered me until now."

Kelsey reached over and patted his hand. "You have the best

instincts of anyone I know. If you say there's something off, then I believe you."

Sawyer grimaced. "I'd just feel better if he was making a podcast about the identified victims and allowing their families to talk about their daughters, sisters, mothers, and wives. But doing an investigative podcast to uncover new victims sounds sexier and is probably far more lucrative."

"You could always make stipulations for your participation," Kelsey suggested. "You already have to set very strict boundaries to protect your professional reputation. Why not throw in a few other caveats, like bonus episodes to highlight the women his father killed? Not all families will want to take part, but there will be friends or coworkers who can give color to their lives."

"That's an excellent idea," Sawyer said. "Beautiful and brilliant."

Kelsey brought both hands to her face and balanced her chin on them. "Thank you." Kelsey liked to joke that only Sawyer recognized her beauty and brains, but that couldn't be further from the truth. And she didn't need or require anyone's adulation because confidence was hard-wired into her DNA, a trait he hoped she would pass on to his and Royce's child.

"Enough shop talk," Kelsey said, waving her hands. "Ready to look at ideas for the nursery?"

A wave of sadness washed over him as Sawyer remembered another time when he'd thought a nursery was in his future. One minute, his life with Vic was as perfect as it could get, and the next, Sawyer was burying his husband and his dreams of fatherhood. In his darkest hours, just getting out of bed required herculean strength, and Sawyer couldn't have imagined the future that waited for him. He was again on the verge of having it all. The intellectual part of his brain knew damn well that the universe wasn't out to get him. The fertility horror stories and the sad memories weren't an omen, and making nursery plans wasn't tempting fate. But his brain's emotional center was in overdrive at the moment, triggering anxiety-driven thoughts that would lead him to really dark places if he let them. So he wouldn't.

Sawyer closed his eyes, took a deep breath, and exhaled it slowly to reset his vagus nerve. He called on all the love, joy, and inner light in his soul to push away the darkness and fear. He imagined a glowing orb expanding and getting brighter until its brilliant light was all he could see. When he reopened his eyes, he met Kelsey's concerned gaze with a reassuring smile. "I'm ready."

"Yeah?"

Sawyer nodded eagerly. "I just had a trippy moment there and needed a reset."

Kelsey held his gaze for a few seconds before scooting her chair closer so they could look at the tablet together. Sawyer had heard of Pinterest, but he'd never explored the site. Kelsey helped him set up an account and showed him how to create a board, mark it as private, and search the site for ideas.

"Oh, wow," Sawyer said. "There are so many things to choose from."

"Don't get overwhelmed. You can pin anything that stands out to you and go back into the board and narrow it down. You can remove pinned items that don't fit or that Royce doesn't like. It's a digital mood board, so you can move things around according to your... mood." They started with the functional things the room needed first. They added different styles of cribs, dressers, armoires, and changing tables to the board.

"You'll want one of these," Kelsey said, pointing to a sunny yellow glider with a matching footstool. "They're perfect for late-night feedings and soothing a little one to sleep." When Sawyer saved it to the collection, Kelsey added, "I didn't mean you had to add this glider. You can get them with just about any fabric color or texture."

"Yeah, I know, but I like the sunny yellow one. It will look great with the pale gray paint, and it reminds me of you."

"Charmer."

"So they say," Sawyer replied as he typed "baby bedding" into the search bar. "Oh, that one," Sawyer said, tapping on the first image featuring a white crib with a baby quilt folded over the edge. Adorable baby safari animals filled each square of the blanket. They were cartoony enough for a nursery without straying too far from the real animals. "I really love this one."

"Add it to the collection, and keep scrolling to see if anything else jumps out at you."

The magnitude and range of nursery themes was impressive and sometimes overwhelming. Sawyer found a few other contenders, but the baby safari animals remained his first pick. Kelsey helped him find storage and decor options that matched the theme, including wall stickers that looked like murals. He just needed to convince Royce.

Sawyer was shocked when he noticed the time. "We've been at this for almost two hours."

"Welcome to the Pinterest rabbit hole. Wait until you explore recipes and life hacks."

"That's probably better than the carpet cleaning videos I got hooked on while I was in Denver," Sawyer told her.

"What? Show me?"

They spent another hour watching his new friend James tackle dirty rugs with his adorably named machines and tools before they moved to the pool. Swimming for Kelsey meant floating on a raft with a cold beverage in her hand and warning people not to get her hair wet. Sawyer enjoyed a dip in the cold water before he hoisted himself on a raft and sipped a virgin strawberry daiquiri he'd whipped up for them in the blender. And that's where Royce found them when he returned home. He'd changed out of his work clothes and put on tropical-themed board shorts and a white tank top. Seeing his husband's handsome face had the same intoxicating effect as the booze he'd left out of the drink.

"Yay!" Kelsey and Sawyer cheered.

Royce smirked as he approached them. He tossed his phone onto a lounger before walking to the edge of the pool. "I could get used to this kind of greeting." He squatted down, reached for Sawyer's float, and tugged him closer. "You look blissful."

"I am. I have the most amazing husband and best friend." Sawyer puckered his lips for a kiss.

Royce eyed him warily but leaned forward. Sawyer grabbed a fistful of his tank top and pulled him into the water.

"Hey now," Kelsey said, holding up her hand as if that would keep her curls dry. "You know the rules."

Royce emerged from the water looking like an aquatic god. He slicked the drenched hair off his forehead and apologized to Kelsey for Sawyer's naughty behavior. "I will teach him a lesson."

"Mm-hmm. I just bet you will, but can it wait? My bestie promised me Mexican food."

Royce held Sawyer's gaze as he said, "Sure thing. Let him worry about his punishment for a few hours."

Worry wasn't causing the tingle of arousal in Sawyer's balls.

Kelsey snorted and paddled closer to the edge of the pool.

"Where are you going?" Sawyer asked.

"I'm going to call Andrew and ask him to meet us at the restaurant. Our little angel is still with Grandma, so we can have an adult double date. Chips, salsa, and all the beans!"

"Lucky Andrew," Royce called after her.

Kelsey acknowledged him with a bark of laughter as she rummaged through her purse for her phone.

"How was your day?" Sawyer asked.

"Boring and frustrating." Royce rested his hands on the raft and pulled it closer when Sawyer started to drift away. "I don't know much more than I did yesterday, so I could've stayed home and enjoyed the day with you." He glanced over at the patio where Kelsey talked on the phone to Andrew. "But I think you had the day you needed."

"You're always my first choice to do anything with, and I'm glad you're home now." Sawyer ran his fingers through Royce's hair. "What's this about a punishment?"

Royce placed a hand on Sawyer's thigh and squeezed. His gray eyes smoldered with an intensity that made Sawyer suck in a sharp breath. "Before dinner, we're going to shower together." Royce trailed his fingers up Sawyer's legs until he reached the bottom of his swim shorts. "I'm going to work you up to the point of painful arousal and refuse to let you come." When Kelsey went inside the house, Royce slipped his fingers under the shorts and brushed them against Sawyer's balls through the mesh liner. "You'll sit across the table from me, primed and ready to fuck, fighting the urge to squirm and give yourself away or make yourself come." Royce slipped his fingers under the mesh netting and cupped Sawyer fully, skin to skin.

"Come?"

Royce dipped his fingers lower, pushing between Sawyer's ass cheeks to tap a finger against his quivering pucker. "Squirming will press the butt plug against your prostate."

The words alone were enough to make Sawyer groan and press against Royce's finger. They hadn't used a plug in a long time, and the prospect of doing so in public sent sharp pangs of arousal straight to his balls. Royce eased his hand free of his swimming trunks, but not before Sawyer's body reacted to the physical and verbal stimulation.

"Can't have that," Royce said, nodding toward Sawyer's semi-erection. "You should cool off." He grabbed the daiquiri with one hand and flipped Sawyer's raft with the other.

Sawyer knew the payback was coming, but he still managed to get water up his nose. He sputtered when he surfaced, reclaimed his fruity drink, and kissed Royce hard on the mouth. "What will you do to me after we get home from dinner?"

Royce gripped Sawyer's ass with both hands and yanked him forward. "You'll just have to wait and find out."

CHAPTER TEN

ROYCE STOPPED AT A RED LIGHT AND LOOKED OVER AT THE passenger seat, where Sawyer half moaned in pleasure and half groaned in dismay from stimulation overload. "Problems?"

Sawyer turned and scowled at him. The red glow from the traffic light covered half of his face, making his expression look sinister. "You didn't tell me the damn butt plug would vibrate when you slipped it inside my ass or that it had settings you could control with a remote."

"You didn't ask," Royce replied with a shrug. "Besides, my mouth was full of your dick at the time, and the thought slipped my mind."

Half of Sawyer's face lit up green, so Royce gave his full attention to the road and hit the gas. His husband growled and rocked his hips in the seat. "A cock ring and a butt plug are too much. Hurts." But then he ruined the complaint with a long, delicious moan. "So good."

"Sounds like one of my favorite songs." Royce reached into his pocket and pressed the up-arrow key on the tiny remote as he sang lines from the John Mellencamp song.

"Fuck. Oh fuck!"

"You want me to fuck off, fuck around, or fuck you?"

A dark laugh rumbled from Sawyer, and he sounded borderline delirious. "Yes. Just yes. Drive faster."

"Speeding is against the law."

Sawyer braced one hand on the dashboard and the other on the side window. He ground his hips, riding the toy with abandon. "I'm going to come without you." He tilted his head back, and his moans turned into needy whimpers. Royce knew the sounds Sawyer made when he was on the verge of orgasm, and he was right there.

Royce turned the vibrations off and earned an angry snarl. "Damned if I do and damned if I don't."

"I might kill you for this."

Royce waggled his brows. "I think the pleasure might kill us both."

They made two more right turns into their neighborhood and one left into their driveway. The garage door had barely rolled up high enough to drive under, but Royce was on a mission. He put the SUV in park, killed the engine, and hit the overhead button to close the door. He didn't wait for complete privacy before he reached for Sawyer. Their seat belts made things difficult, so they unbuckled them and exited the car as fast as they could, meeting at the hood of the SUV with hungry mouths and roaming hands.

"Fuck me. Fuck me right now," Sawyer said in between kisses. "Bend me over the hood."

"You're not in charge, remember?"

Sawyer closed his eyes and whined. "You've punished me enough for one night."

Royce nipped a path along his neck and guided him to the door. "I'll decide when it's enough."

They stumbled into the house, banging the door into the wall hard enough to knock the decorative key holder to the floor. Instead of fixing it, Royce tossed his set onto the mess and kept guiding Sawyer sideways. He reached into his pocket and removed the little remote.

"Don't you d—"

Sawyer gasped when Royce powered up the vibration on the plug, and his eyes rolled back in his head a little. Sawyer whimpered and attacked Royce's mouth with a savagery that knocked Royce back a step until he recovered and seized control again, clumsily steering his husband through the house. They bumped into a stool and knocked something off the kitchen island onto the floor. It didn't involve shattered glass, so Royce kept going. Sawyer's foot caught on the living room rug, and they both nearly toppled to the ground. Sawyer laughed as he righted himself, and Royce decided he had to have him right then.

Royce made quick work of loosening Sawyer's belt and opening his pants. One good tug and the fabric pooled at Sawyer's ankles, leaving him in tight white briefs. The head of his dick had leaked enough cum to make a large transparent circle on the fabric. Royce dropped to his knees, tonguing the wet spot and moaning when he got a taste of Sawyer. Hands fisted in his hair, dragging his face closer, but Royce only used the tip of his tongue to drive his husband into a higher state of arousal.

"Something is about to burst," Sawyer growled.

Royce sat back on his haunches and stared up at his husband. He'd removed his shirt and tossed it somewhere, leaving his gorgeously toned body mostly bare. "You're about to bust a nut on this rug when I bend you over and fuck you."

Sawyer couldn't get free from his shoes, socks, and pants fast enough. Royce worried he'd fall and helped him undress before he injured something vital. Sawyer wrapped a fist around his dick and stroked. His balls looked taut and ready to blow from being restricted. "Better h-hurry."

Royce tugged Sawyer's hand away from his dick. "Get on your knees, then."

While Sawyer got into position, Royce stripped off his shirt, shucked his pants and underwear down his legs, and located the bottle of lube hidden in the living room. He turned and found Sawyer on his hands and knees with his legs spread and his ass pushed out and presented for Royce's pleasure. What in the hell had he done to deserve this man? He'd probably never have an answer to the question and decided it wasn't the right time to ponder life's biggest mysteries when its biggest pleasure awaited.

Royce dropped to his knees behind his husband and leaned over his back. Sawyer whimpered when Royce's dick pressed against his ass, and he trembled when Royce settled his hand on Sawyer's chest. Curious fingers snaked a path down his belly, swirled in the sticky mess his precum had made before nudging the head of his engorged dick.

"I need you," Sawyer moaned.

"You have me." Placing a kiss between tense shoulders, Royce eased up so he could attend to Sawyer's ass first. He gripped the handle of the plug and gave it a little nudge to make Sawyer buck into the pleasure. "Easy now," Royce urged as he gently twisted and wiggled the plug free. He dropped the toy to the rug, and Royce took his time tracing the flexing pucker. "I'm going to fill you and fuck you without mercy."

"Finally," Sawyer whined.

Royce slapped his ass cheek to remind him who was in charge, but his dick ached too much to drag this foreplay out much longer. He coated his dick with lube, lined it up, and plunged inside Sawyer's snug heat on a triumphant shout. He'd wanted to go slow and draw out their pleasure, but they were both too far gone. Royce went to work, pounding the sweetest ass in existence. When his orgasm loomed near, he released the cock ring from Sawyer's balls. One more deep thrust and

Sawyer spilled all over the rug, his ass clamping tighter around Royce's dick with every spurt. The orgasm hit like a Mack truck, and Royce pumped his release inside Sawyer, holding him tight as if he might try to escape. They collapsed to the rug and quickly rolled over once Sawyer landed in the mess he'd made. They lay on their sides, staring into one another's eyes as they came down off their high.

"That was insane," Sawyer said between pants.

"Same time next week?" Royce asked.

Laughing, Sawyer rolled his husband onto his back and kissed him soundly. "Maybe we don't involve the unsuspecting public. We live in this community, and it won't do either of our reputations any good if you're caught holding the remote after I jizz my pants in public."

Royce snorted before giving in to a full-body laugh. "Fair enough. We'll wait until we go out of town."

"Deal," Sawyer said before nuzzling his nose into Royce's neck. "We need showers. I feel like I'm covered in cum."

"Just a little here and there."

"You know how fussy I am."

Royce rubbed his hand through the mess, smearing it into Sawyer's skin. "While I love getting you dirty."

They moved to the bathroom, where they continued necking and petting in the shower. Afterward, Royce left Sawyer to lounge in bed to watch television while he fixed the key holder, cleaned the cum off the carpet, and retrieved their clothes. His phone fell out of his pocket when he lifted his jeans, and Royce saw a text notification. His brain was too scattered from sex to recognize its importance until he opened the thread and read the message.

He and Diego had spent their day trying to track down the Matisse's household staff, only to come up empty. They'd discovered that the chef, Ricardo Ramirez, had gone out of town on a short cruise with his boyfriend. The couple's chatty neighbor said the men had been planning the cruise for over a year, so they hadn't fled the country to cover up a crime or avoid talking to him. Trying to find Yvonne Miller, the Matisses' full-time housekeeper, had been a different story altogether. She lived in a neighborhood that didn't trust cops, so they weren't willing to discuss where she might be.

Royce had left voicemail messages and texted her a few times, but she hadn't responded all day. And he understood why she would be hesitant to talk to them about the Matisse family. Even if she hadn't witnessed anything nefarious, just talking to the police could jeopardize future employment with clients like the Matisse family. Wealthy folks liked to protect their privacy, and Yvonne wouldn't want to get a reputation as someone with loose lips. But the housekeeper had finally responded and agreed to speak with them in the morning at a neutral location away from the Matisse home. After a quick text exchange, they agreed to meet at Bytes and Brew at seven thirty in the morning.

Royce updated Diego on the latest development and let out an excited whoop, certain Yvonne would have good intel on that family. Mind-bending sex followed by a potential break in the case called for a celebration, and ice cream sundaes sounded like the perfect way to cap off a wonderful evening. Royce dropped the dirty clothes and retreated into the kitchen to whip up a sweet treat, and that's when he noticed the paper bag with a bakery logo and what appeared to be pastry crumbs all over the floor.

"What are you whooping it up about in here?" Sawyer asked as he strolled into the kitchen in a pair of loose-fitting cotton pants.

Just like that, Royce's brain was temporarily distracted. "Damn, I like the way your dick looks in those PJs."

Sawyer snorted. "There's no way you have any gas left in the tank."

Royce shrugged. "Doesn't stop me from noticing and admiring perfection when I see it." He lifted the paper bag. "What was in here?"

Sawyer narrowed his eyes. "Croissants. Kelsey brought over half a dozen this morning. We each ate one and shared a third. You didn't sniff them out when you got home?"

Royce shook his head. "I can't believe my nose failed me." He pointed to the crumbs on the floor. A trail led into the utility room, where they kept the pet food bowls. "I think we knocked the bag off the table when we stumbled into the house, and I bet I know who ate the final three croissants while we were fucking like porn stars on the rug."

The trail of buttery pastry crumbs led them straight to their thieving cat and dog, who stared up at them with innocent eyes.

Meow. Bones' denial dislodged a hunk of pastry off one of his whiskers.

Yip, yip, yip. Dolly's bouncing barks sent a flurry of tiny flakes to the ground like a French pastry snowfall.

"Holy shit," Sawyer said. "I better call Kelsey and see what other flavors she purchased in case any of the ingredients were toxic. I know they didn't eat any chocolate, lavender, or honey."

"Lavender?" Royce scoffed. "The flower?"

"It's a delicacy."

"For birds and bees, maybe."

"Be right back." Sawyer darted from the room, and Royce heard the concern in his voice when he called Kelsey.

"Bad kids. Bad, bad kids," Royce told them. "Your shenanigans might cause a trip the v-e-t." Dolly would hate it, but Bones would soak up the adoration faster than they'd wolfed down the croissants.

Sawyer darted back into the utility room. "We're in the clear. None of the other ingredients were toxic, but they might get upset stomachs from all the butter, so we're not out of the woods completely."

"You two aren't gassing us out of our room tonight. You can sleep in your beds in the living room."

"Yeah, what he said," Sawyer told them.

"I'm going to make a bowl of ice cream. Do you want some frozen yogurt?"

"Yeah, but just a little. No toppings. I've indulged too much this weekend."

"Watch it, or you'll end up sleeping in the living room with Bones and Dolly."

Sawyer laughed and followed Royce into the kitchen, where he picked up Royce's tablet off the counter. "Kels helped me put together some design ideas for the nursery. Do you want to look at them and give me your thoughts?"

A warmth washed over Royce. It wasn't just from the sappy look on his husband's face or the gooey way Sawyer made him feel inside. It was the totality of the life they'd built and the dreams they were chasing. Royce cupped his neck and pulled him in for a hug. "Forget the ice cream. Show me your nursery ideas."

CHAPTER ELEVEN

ROYCE WOKE TWO HOURS BEFORE HIS ALARM WAS DUE TO GO off. He lay there in the dark, listening for sounds to explain why he'd transitioned from sound asleep to wide-awake as if someone had flipped a switch in his brain. Their bedroom and the house beyond were completely quiet, aside from the soft breathing coming from his husband and roommates. He'd talked a tough game the previous night, but Bones and Dolly had still slept with them. Royce would need to work on effective discipline skills for fatherhood. The pets practically laughed in his face when he laid down the law, and he didn't want to get the same reaction from a teenager someday.

He closed his eyes and willed himself to sleep, but to no avail. His brain was doing mental jumping jacks, and the rest of him either needed to catch up, or he'd feel out of sync for the rest of the day. If his mind was going to race a mile a minute, he should hit the treadmill and try to catch it. Royce eased from the bed, careful not to wake Sawyer or their pets, and slipped into the bathroom to pee and brush his teeth. A full bladder and foul breath were not things he wanted to take with him on a run. He navigated their dark bedroom to remove underwear, socks, and a pair of shorts from his dresser but didn't put them on until he stepped into the hallway and shut the bedroom door behind him. His running shoes and earbuds waited for him in the workout room, so he was ready to go after a quick stretch. Royce snagged a bottle of water from the mini fridge and hit the treadmill. He cranked up the music to drown out any intrusive thoughts and gave himself over to the movement his body craved. Royce much preferred weightlifting to cardio, but sometimes he just needed to stretch his legs like Forrest Gump.

He received an email notification on his phone somewhere around Montana and slowed the treadmill to a quick walk so he could cool down. But then Royce nearly tripped over his own two feet when he saw the email had come from the medical examiner's office. Dr. Fawkes had new updates on the Matisse investigation. Royce turned off the machine and rode the belt like an escalator, stepping down when he ran out of room. He dropped onto the weight bench and logged in to the secure account to read his SPD emails. His smile grew with every result he read. The fingerprints on the pill bottle belonged to Julia and Alyssa. Julia hadn't touched the liquor decanter or tumbler, but her prints were all over the smoothie glass and the spice grinder where the benzodiazepine residue was found. Julia had put the ground pills into her father's green smoothie. Mommy dearest came along a while later and drove the final nail into his coffin when she plied him with scotch.

To be fair, she might've been telling the truth when she claimed to have only poured him one drink. But the doctor either continued drinking on his own, or someone had helped him achieve dangerous blood alcohol levels. What Royce needed to know was if Alyssa Matisse knew her daughter had slipped drugs into his smoothie. He searched the side effects someone might experience while taking benzodiazepine and read that the drug could cause extreme irritability in some people. It was possible and maybe even plausible that Alyssa had simply tried to calm her husband down with a drink and a suggestion he should do an activity he enjoyed. She came across as a woman who staunchly supported her husband, but that could've been an act. Having the irrefutable evidence didn't immediately solve the case like it did on television. Royce would need to interview both women if he hoped to get to the truth, and they'd made it clear he'd need a warrant to do so.

"You asked for it, ladies," Royce said to an empty room.

He smiled gleefully as he dialed Diego's number. The young detective answered with a snarl. "Rise and shine, D. The Matisse case just caught fire, and we have a lot of work to do."

Yvonne Miller's soft brown eyes darted around Bytes and Brew as if searching for signs of the Boogeyman or one of the Matisse women. Royce was absolutely certain neither of them had even heard of the cybercafé, let alone stepped inside it. The woman practically vibrated with nerves, and he hated to cause her additional stress. Contrary to what he'd thought, Yvonne hadn't been avoiding him on purpose. She'd explained in her text that she worked three jobs to support herself and her aging parents.

"We won't keep you long," Royce assured her. He already had enough information to obtain his warrants, so whatever she told them would just be icing on the cake.

"Thank you," Yvonne replied. "I can't afford to be late."

"Would you like a cup of coffee?" Diego asked.

Yvonne looked longingly at the menu, dropped her gaze, and shook her head.

Diego leaned forward and lowered his voice. "It will be my treat."

Yvonne lifted her head. "Are you sure?"

Diego aimed his megawatt smile at her. "I might have to do some extra dishes or something." At Yvonne's confused expression, he winked. "My husband is the owner. Why don't I sweet-talk him out of a couple of brews while you guys get started?"

"You know my order," Royce said.

Yvonne ordered a salted caramel latte that made him think of Sawyer. His face must've betrayed his brain's detour—most likely a dopey smile—because Yvonne asked if it was his favorite drink.

"No, but it's an indulgence my husband can't refuse."

Yvonne seemed to relax after that. She rested her hands on the table and squared her shoulders. "What would you like to know about Dr. and Mrs. Matisse?"

As Royce considered the best way to phrase his questions, it occurred to him that he was most curious about Julia. Maybe Alyssa Matisse had fooled him with her unwavering support for her husband, but of the two women, Julia seemed more impulsive and volatile. Was duress to blame for her behavior, or had the traumatic events exposed her true nature? She was the one who'd ground the benzos into a powder and slipped it into her father's protein smoothie. Julia Matisse was the one with the daddy issues. What Royce needed to prove was her intention. When had she drugged her father? Had she tried to kill him? It sounded like Dr. Matisse was a hard man to live with, but what pushed her over the edge? Had she overheard her father's conversations with Felix or Richard Todd on Friday? If what Julia told him was correct, Yvonne had already left by the time Dr.

Matisse had spoken with either man. Verifying what time the staff left would be a good place to start.

"What time did you and Ricardo leave on Friday?" Royce asked as Diego returned with their coffee.

Yvonne took a sip from the cup, and a blissful expression washed over her face. Then she set the coffee down and fixed them with a serious gaze. "Ricardo finished food prep for the long weekend and left around ten. Mrs. Matisse had asked me to tackle some extra cleaning projects last week, and I finished them up right around noon. I looked for Mrs. Matisse to see if there was anything else she needed, but she'd left the house for an appointment. Julia told me I could leave. She doesn't sign my paychecks, and I wasn't sure I should listen. I asked if I should speak with Dr. Matisse first, but she laughed and said he didn't get involved with domestic operations. Julia said he likely didn't know my name." Yvonne frowned and shook her head. "I've worked for the family since they moved to Savannah, and that really hurt my feelings."

"I bet," Royce said.

"It was a terribly rude thing to say," Diego added.

Yvonne smiled sadly. "But also likely true, so I didn't feel guilty about cutting out early. I don't get a lot of time for myself. I was eager to enjoy it and ran right out of there without my purse." She shook her head. "I went back inside to retrieve it from the utility room." Yvonne lowered her head for a few minutes before looking up to meet Royce's gaze. "That's when I heard the shouting."

"Who was shouting?"

"Dr. Matisse. His voice was muffled, and I could tell he was in his office. The conversation was one-sided, so I knew he was on the phone. I'd never known him to yell at himself, and Julia would've been giving it right back if he'd shouted at her like that."

160

"Can you recall anything that was said?" Royce asked.

Yvonne's face turned pink, and she averted her eyes again.

"There's nothing to be embarrassed about," he said. "It's human nature to be curious."

Yvonne slowly lifted her gaze. "I tried to creep closer to find out what was going on, but I saw Julia standing outside his office door. Dr. Matisse was still yelling, but all my attention was on her. She'd gone as rigid as a board and as white as a ghost. Julia had one hand pressed against her stomach and the other covering her mouth. She didn't move or make a sound. Julia looked like grief had turned her to stone. The only sign of life was the silent tears sliding down her face. I felt terrible for her. If she'd ever shown an ounce of warmth in her personality, I might've gone to her and offered comfort."

"What did you do?" Royce asked.

"I turned and left as quietly as I could."

"You don't think she saw you?" Diego asked.

Yvonne shook her head. "I'm not even sure she was aware of her surroundings."

"And you can't recall a single word Dr. Matisse shouted?"

Yvonne pursed her lips and scrunched her brow for a few seconds before shaking her head. "It wasn't the words that caught my attention. It was his voice. Dr. Matisse has always been quick to anger and blustery, but this was unlike anything I'd ever heard from him. He sounded like his world was about to end, and he was desperate to stop it."

"It's impossible for you to know how much of the conversation Julia overheard, correct?" Royce clarified.

"That's right. I just know she was already listening outside his door when I approached at the end of the hallway, and she was still there when I decided my paycheck meant more to me than being nosy."

"Have you been in touch with Alyssa or Julia since Dr. Matisse's death?"

Yvonne nodded. "I called Mrs. Matisse as soon as I heard the news on Saturday evening. She didn't answer my call, so I left her a voicemail message. I offered my condolences and asked her to call if she needed anything from me. I thought she might need me to clean, call the pool company, or prepare food for visitors. They have so many friends, and I expected them to swarm Mrs. Matisse to offer comfort and support. But she didn't get back to me." Yvonne worked her bottom lip between her teeth. "Then I saw the paper on Sunday and realized why. The accusations in that article would've destroyed her. Mrs. Matisse is a proud woman and wouldn't want anyone to see her vulnerabilities. She will refuse to believe her husband was capable of those things because of what it might say about her."

"Would you say Dr. Matisse and Mrs. Matisse had a good marriage?" Diego asked.

"What's a good marriage these days?" Yvonne asked with a dry chuckle. "Their relationship was intense and sometimes volatile. I wouldn't say they were in love, and I'm not even sure they liked each other very much. They didn't laugh or spend time together when I was there. Maybe they became an entirely different couple after I went home each day."

Royce somehow doubted that. "Did any of the volatility ever lead to physical violence?"

"No," she said slowly, "but I would say Dr. Matisse could be emotionally abusive. Especially regarding Julia. Nothing she did pleased either of them, but Mrs. Matisse at least attempted to go through the motions of being a supportive parent. Dr. Matisse ridiculed Julia horribly when she was younger, and she'd developed an eating disorder. They argued viciously for years, and then Julia became nearly as invisible to Dr. Matisse as the household help. This weekend is the first time she's returned to Savannah in years."

"That's really sad." Royce would be the first person to admit his daddy issues, and he clocked them in other people too. "I have nothing else to ask right now." Royce looked at Diego to see if he had more questions to ask, but he just shook his head. "I'll do everything I can to leave you out of this investigation, but what you witnessed might end up being very important."

Yvonne exhaled her next breath slowly. "Don't worry about me, Sergeant Locke. Clients like the Matisses will beat down my door to hire me if they think I have gossip to share. They're nothing more than vultures who won't stop until they've picked the carcasses clean. They hide behind high-end clothes, expensive jewelry, and genteel manners to conceal their gory activities." She pushed back her chair and stood. "I'll make an official report if you need me to."

Royce rose to his feet and shook her hand. "I appreciate it."

She thanked Diego for the coffee and hurried from the café. They waited for her to disappear down the sidewalk before heading out too.

"What do you think?" Royce asked once they were in his SUV.

"I think both Matisse women had strong motives to want Jean Claude Matisse dead." Diego considered. "If Alyssa Matisse participated in his death, wouldn't she accept Yvonne's offer to clean up? That would've destroyed the evidence, and we wouldn't have a case."

"That's a sound argument someone thinking rationally would make, but murder is usually triggered by high emotions that result in mistakes." Royce looked out the windshield as he mentally moved the puzzle pieces around to form a clear picture. "We don't have a reason to doubt what Yvonne told us, and the timing of the phone call matches what we learned from Felix and Richard Todd. So, Jean Claude got into a shouting match on the phone around noon on Friday. Alyssa Matisse wasn't home, but Julia was."

"And Yvonne placed a stricken Julia right outside her father's office during the phone call," Diego said. "How do you want to play this?"

Royce glanced at his watch. "Let's cross our t's and dot our i's because we're going to keep our nine o'clock appointment with the Matisse women."

CHAPTER TWELVE

SAWYER KNOCKED ON MENDOZA'S DOOR AND RECEIVED A prompt command to enter the office, so he turned the knob and stepped into the room. Though the chief sat behind his desk and his husband, Sheriff Abe Beecham, sat in a chair on the other side, Sawyer couldn't help but feel like he'd interrupted something personal. "Is this a bad time, Chief?"

The two men looked at one another, a mere glance, but he caught a flash of heat between them. Yeah, he'd definitely interrupted an intimate moment or conversation between husbands. Probably the kind of chat Royce coerced Sawyer into behind his closed office door, which usually included a lot of kissing and some light petting. He refused to search for further signs of what the two men might've been up to before he knocked.

Chief Mendoza's dark, penetrating eyes zeroed in on Sawyer. "If I'd been busy, I would've said so instead of inviting you in."

Abe snorted. "Invite? More like you barked a direct order."

Mendoza ignored his husband and gestured for Sawyer to take a seat. "You wanted to speak to us about a meeting you had with Alec Bishop?"

"Yes, sir."

Sawyer filled them in on the conversation he'd had with Alec and the ties his family had to the area. "The first murder connected to Andrew Bishop occurred when his father was forty years old. We're all familiar with various theories about serial killers and the profiles performed on them. One of the common denominators in their behavior sequence analysis is that they start killing young, usually in their mid to late twenties. Of course there are exceptions, but according to Alec, his father ticks off all boxes in the 'How to Make a Serial Killer' checklist. He actually uses that phrase when talking about his father's history, particularly the trauma and abuse he suffered as a kid."

"And Alec hypothesizes that if his father has met all the other markers, then he likely fit the starts-young criteria too," Mendoza said.

"It's not a gigantic leap," Abe admitted. "We've got the tools at our disposal to sort through unsolved cases and pinpoint ones that fit the criteria. Did Alec tell you when his family lived in Chatham County?"

"Yes, sir. I entered the dates into SPD's database and came up with five potential matches. They're all unsolved murders of young women. Three had positive identifications, and the other two are listed as Jane Does. All five were exposed to harsh elements for significant time, and our chances of getting conclusive test results from the biological evidence are low."

Mendoza steepled his fingers in front of his chest as he considered the situation. "You think it's a long shot?"

"I do," Sawyer agreed, "but Alec Bishop has raised a lot of money for this project and will guarantee the funding for any testing."

"What's in it for him?" Abe asked.

"Book deals, speaking tours, and probably a Netflix series," Mendoza said.

Abe scowled. "Fame and money, then."

"But if we're successful, we could get closure for the families without straining our department's budget," Sawyer said. "It's hard to find a downside to the proposal."

"He could make our departments look like idiots," Abe replied.

"True, but I already mentioned that concern to him," Sawyer said. "He will offer editing approval for any departmental interviews he includes in the podcast or that he makes available to subscribers through bonus material on Patreon."

"I'm okay with transparency," Mendoza said, "even if it shines a negative light on past investigations our police department had conducted." He held Sawyer's gaze for several seconds and tapped the tips of his fingers together. "Have his people call our people."

"And who are our people?" Sawyer asked.

Mendoza chuckled. "Hell if I know. Have Mr. Bishop write up a detailed proposal, and I'll personally deliver it to Commissioner Rigby. She'll consult with our legal department, and we'll go from there."

Sawyer thanked Mendoza before turning to the sheriff. "And you, sir?"

Abe nodded toward his husband. "What he said. Bishop needs to put a formal proposal and email it to hot top cop at CCSD—" Abe's words died mid-sentence when he ducked from the Tootsie Roll Mendoza lobbed at him. "You'll pay for that."

"Promises, promises."

It was a carefree side of the men Sawyer had never seen before, and he sat there staring at their interaction until an awkward silence fell over the room. Mendoza arched a brow in silent question.

"Um, yeah," Sawyer said. "That's all I needed."

He exited as quickly as he could and strode back to his office. Sawyer opened his phone calendar, where he'd noted Alec's contact information, and saw the entry for the fertility clinic appointment.

Instead of firing off an email to share the update with Alec, Sawyer stared at his phone. He remembered the conversation with Kelsey and her suggestion to call Dr. Flores to put his worries about the insemination to rest. He dialed the clinic before he could talk himself out of it. A receptionist answered on the second ring. He expected the staff to sound harried and frustrated, but the woman was calm and sympathetic as Sawyer stated his reason for calling.

"Can I place you on a brief hold?" she asked.

"Of course. Thank you."

Sawyer expected someone else to come on the line, an assistant or a nurse, but Dr. Flores greeted him warmly a few minutes later. She understood why he'd called but didn't rush him or try to guide the conversation. After Sawyer finished explaining his concerns, she patiently described the safety protocols her clinic followed to prevent accidental errors.

"And I assure you, I've only acted with a hundred percent integrity," Dr. Flores said. "If the allegations against Dr. Matisse are proven true, then he acted in the most egregious way. I'd never betray my patients like that. If Friday's insemination was successful, and I do like your odds, the paternity of your child will match the choice you and Royce made at the clinic. And that's a guarantee."

A montage of beautiful images flickered across Sawyer's mind, not a home movie of experiences he'd already lived but snapshots of what his future would look like. Royce and their child were at the heart of every one. He imagined his husband cradling their baby for the first time, rocking them to sleep while telling outlandish stories, dancing with their toddler in the kitchen, and picking out school supplies that were functional and fun. Everything Sawyer had been bold enough to dream was on the verge of coming true and—

"Sawyer, are you still there?" Dr. Flores asked.

Her voice snapped him back to reality, and he blinked a few times to bring his office into focus. Sawyer's vision remained blurry, and that was when he realized his face was wet. He chuckled nervously as he rubbed his eyes with his free hand. "Yes, I'm still here. Thank you so much for your time and your assurances."

"My pleasure. I'll see you at the pregnancy blood test in ten days."

"Yes, ma'am."

After they said their goodbyes, Sawyer leaned back in his chair and closed his eyes. He let peace wash over him and chase away negative and scary thoughts surrounding the potential pregnancy or paternity concerns. Finding faith in a chaotic world felt like throwing himself out of an airplane without a parachute, grasping and clawing for anything to keep himself from hurtling toward his death. It was a free fall of mind fuckery, giving him a false sense of well-being one minute, only to jerk it back when the lifesaving parachute was nothing more than a mirage. Sawyer knew all too well how precarious and precious life was. He'd loved and lost. Floated like a feather and plummeted like a rock. Sawyer had dreamed and failed. Then he dared to love again. Why would anyone set themselves up for such nauseating risks? How could they not? The highest highs weren't possible without the lowest lows, and knowing he didn't leap alone made the risk worth it.

A phone rang in the cold case squad room and snapped him back to reality. He'd gotten so caught up in the imagery of free-falling that his stomach lurched as if he'd just landed in the chair, and Sawyer would've sworn his hair even rustled in the breeze. Then he heard the familiar rattle from the air-conditioning vent above his desk and laughed at himself. As much as he'd love to get lost in daydreams, he needed to focus on work. He found Alec Bishop's email address and typed a brief message, asking him to call when it was convenient. Sawyer debated whether to add his cell phone number or just use his direct line at the SPD. He went with the latter since there was no valid reason for Alec to call him outside his office hours. Sawyer hit Send and was surprised when his desk phone rang almost immediately.

"This is Detective Sergeant Key," he said.

"Hi, it's Alec." His voice was soft but eager, just as Sawyer remembered from their private chat.

"That was fast," Sawyer said. Too fast, or were Royce's doubts getting to him?

"I was scrolling through my inbox when your message hit. It was a convenient time for me to call, so I did. Is this a good time for you to talk?"

"Sure. I just came out of a meeting with my police chief and the county sheriff after doing a preliminary search for cases that could meet your father's MO."

"Wow. You didn't waste any time. Did you find any potential matches?"

"I only have access to SPD's cold cases, but I identified five that have all the right markers. I told Chief Mendoza and Sheriff Beecham about your intentions, and they were willing to discuss the opportunity further."

Alec snorted. "Meaning there are hoops to jump through and hurdles to leap over. Do they realize how much funding I can provide?"

"I did point that out, but you also have to understand that our legal department will have to approve participation."

Alec sighed heavily. "Fine."

"You're welcome to investigate these cases without our help," Sawyer said calmly.

"That's not what I want at all. I'm a team player, and I'll prove it to you. How does your chief and his husband want me to proceed?"

The question gave Sawyer pause. He hadn't told Alec that Mendoza and Beecham were married. It was common knowledge locally, but outsiders would only know if they'd researched the men. Alec must've read into Sawyer's delayed response because he chuckled.

"Come on," Alec said. "I did my homework on all the key players in Savannah before I pitched my idea to you at the convention. So hit me with their demands."

"They just want you to send a formal proposal so they can submit it to the proper channels for approval." Sawyer paused as he remembered the grievances he shared with Kelsey. "And I also have a caveat."

"You do?" The question almost came out like a purr. Was Alec flirting with him? If he'd truly done his research, then he'd know about Royce. "Hit me with it."

Sawyer paused to consider his phrasing, then decided he didn't care. Part of him wanted Alec to call the whole thing off. "I would like you to honor your father's known victims. They've been left out of the narrative, and I think it's unfair and just plain wrong."

"That's never been my intention," Alec said contritely. "I'm open to suggestions."

"Dedicate episodes to the victims. Sit down with the people who loved them most so they can share who these women were."

"Interesting," Alec said. "Tell me more."

"Some podcasts release this type of content at the conclusion of a season, and others pepper them in between episodes of the current investigation. You could either extend the season or release two shows each week. Some podcasts would include this type of material in their Patreon feed."

"I don't want to seem like I'm profiting off their deaths," Alec said. "That's the main reason I've kept the focus on my dad's story."

Sawyer could argue that there wouldn't be a story without the victims, but he wanted to give Alec the benefit of the doubt. "So put the bonus episodes in the regular feed or promise to donate the subscription revenue to victims' advocacy groups."

Alec sucked in a breath. "Damn, you're good. I better hope you don't take my idea and run with it on your own."

Chuckling, Sawyer shook his head before he remembered Alec couldn't see him. "You don't have to worry about that. I have no desire to take on additional projects, nor will I have the time." Those images of Royce with their future baby flashed in his mind again, and Sawyer felt dizzy with happiness.

"You'll be otherwise engaged?" Alec pressed.

"You could say that." And that was all he planned to say on the matter. "Write up your proposal and send it to us. We'll have our legal departments review it, and we'll go from there. Maybe we could do a Zoom call between the principal parties."

"I'll have the proposals ready in a day or so and will be in touch."

"Sounds good."

Sawyer couldn't say he was fully convinced working with Alec Bishop was a good idea, but he felt better about it after their conversation. His cell phone chimed with an incoming text from his husband. *Have warrants. Going back out to the Matisses' home. Hope to wrap this case up soon. xo*

Sawyer tapped out a quick reply. *Can't wait to hear all about it. Be careful.* <3

Some might dismiss socialites as dangerous, but they made drag queens seem like tame kittens when things didn't go their way. Besides, if Royce had warrants, he suspected one or more of them of murder or manslaughter, depending on their intent. People with dark secrets have proven they're willing to go to extreme lengths to keep them buried. Royce had a reputation for being a wild card when Sawyer joined the police department, but it hadn't taken him long to see the label as nothing more than camouflage. Royce was an aggressive pursuer of justice, but he didn't cross lines or carelessly put lives in jeopardy, which was good since they were going to become fathers. And just like that, Sawyer got lost in the daydreams of what would be.

CHAPTER THIRTEEN

ROYCE PUSHED THE MATISSES' DOORBELL AND ROCKED BACK on his heels. "I've never had a big dénouement in a mansion before. It makes me feel like a fictional detective, like Hercule Poirot." He ran his fingers over the smooth skin above his upper lip. "Do you think I'd look good with a mustache?"

"Ew. No," Diego said with an offensive cringe.

"Okay. You don't have to be cruel. A simple no would suffice."

Diego shook his head. "And what's a dénouement?"

Had Royce butchered the French pronunciation as poorly as Diego? "You're so uncouth." He repeated it the way Sawyer said, or at least tried.

"And you think you say that any better? What the fuck ever, Masterpiece Theater," Diego quipped. "Is the dénouement the big reveal at the end of murder mystery movies and books?"

"Yep." Royce jammed his finger against the doorbell button again and scowled. Had Yvonne said something that tipped off Julia and Alyssa? Nah. The security guard said neither woman had left the premises. They could've hired a helicopter to pick them up, but that would've likely gotten back to the security team. He rang the doorbell again for good measure. They would regret keeping him waiting.

"I say it was Miss Julia, in the kitchen, with the tainted smoothie," Diego said.

The large wooden double doors flew open before Royce could respond. Yvonne stared at them with wide eyes. "C-c-can I help you?"

"We have arrest warrants for Alyssa and Julia Matisse," Royce told her. "Can you please take us to them?"

Yvonne's mouth dropped open, and she blinked several times before she pulled herself together and stepped aside for them to enter.

"This is the first time we've met," Royce whispered to her as he stepped inside the house. He turned and gave a thumbs-up to the patrol car that waited in front of the house to provide additional transportation.

"They're in the salon," Yvonne said. "Do you know the way?"

"We do. Thank you."

They entered the sitting room as quietly as they could, more to observe what was going on than to catch them admitting something they wouldn't want the police to hear. Richard Todd and Alyssa sat close together on the velvet settee. Some might say too close for a grieving widow, but he knew people dealt with loss in various and sometimes mysterious ways. Alyssa's hand rested just above Richard's knee, and he covered it with his own. There was nothing enigmatic about the expression on the man's face. He was deeply in love with the woman sitting beside him.

Julia sat motionless across from them in the chair Royce had used during their first interview. Her wavy hair cascaded over her shoulders, and she wore a frilly black dress that made her skin look sickly pale. She'd put on a vibrant shade of lipstick and dotted pink blush on her fair cheeks in nearly perfect circles. Julia looked like a life-sized

Victorian porcelain doll that had been cast aside and forgotten while the others conversed quietly in the room.

Royce cleared his throat to announce their presence. Julia was the first to react, leaping to her bare feet so fast that her long skirt swished around her ankles. Anger flushed her skin until the rest of her face matched her blush. "What are you doing here?" Julia's voice crackled with the same rage flashing in her eyes. She was very much alive now.

"It's nine o'clock on Tuesday morning," Royce replied. "We had an appointment. Did you forget?" He held up his phone, pressed a button, and added, "I'm going to record this conversation." He rattled off the date, time, and attendees.

Richard and Alyssa rose to their feet, albeit much slower and without an outward show of any emotion.

"Sergeant," Richard said, "I believe Alyssa and Julia explicitly said they would not speak to you without a warrant."

"Yes, sir, they did," Royce said, pulling the warrants from his back pocket and holding them up for him to see.

Julia jerked her head in Richard's direction and took two aggressive steps toward him before pulling herself together. She stopped suddenly, placed a palm against her sternum, and inhaled a deep breath, which she held for several seconds before releasing it. Julia lowered her hand to her side and addressed Richard in a modulated tone. "You said everything would be okay. You promised us."

The attorney bounced a nervous glance between the Matisse women, Royce, and Diego. "There must be a mistake."

"No, sir. We're here to arrest Alyssa Matisse and Julia Matisse for involuntary manslaughter, though DA Babineaux could bring additional charges as the investigation continues."

"Manslaughter!" Alyssa cried.

"What additional charges?" Julia asked.

"Murder in the first degree," Diego said. "Right now, we're going to assume that neither you nor your mother planned to kill Dr. Matisse and acted independently of one another when you put the benzodiazepine in his smoothie and your mother gave him alcohol. If the evidence shows that you acted together, then the district attorney reserves the right to recharge you."

"What evidence do you even have?" Richard asked. "You mentioned something about fingerprints on glasses. Who cares? Anyone in this house could've handled the dishes at any time."

"We have proof that Julia ground up her mother's prescription benzodiazepine pills in the spice grinder and mixed them into Dr. Matisse's green smoothie," Diego replied. "There was a residue in the grinder cup, the smoothie blender, and the cup Dr. Matisse drank from. The evidence is irrefutable."

Richard scoffed. "We'll just see about that."

"Why is there a warrant for my arrest?" Alyssa asked.

"The pills alone weren't enough to kill him," Royce replied. "But they could account for the extreme irritability and agitation you described. Those are just two negative side effects some people experience while taking benzodiazepine. Mixing the pills with the alcohol is what triggered the respiratory and cardiac failure."

"I didn't know *she* drugged him," Alyssa said. "I thought the scotch would calm him down."

"Mother!" Julia cried out. "How could you turn on me?"

"You'll need to convince the DA of that and possibly a jury," Royce told her.

"Jury?" Alyssa turned to Richard. "I can't go to jail."

Richard took both her hands in his. "You won't, dear. I'll see to it."

"What about me?" Julia asked. "Or do I need to get down on my knees and blow you too?"

Alyssa marched across the short distance and slapped her daughter's face hard enough to rattle her teeth. "Shut your mouth, you ungrateful brat."

Julia covered her face, and the room hung in suspense for all of five seconds before she launched herself at her mother, fisting both hands in Alyssa's hair.

"Oh shit," Diego said, jumping into the melee to pull the women apart. He cuffed Julia and set her in the club chair. Royce tossed his cuffs at Diego, and he secured Alyssa before placing her on the settee. The two women glared at one another, breathing heavily but not speaking. Diego remained between them in case they went for each other again.

"I also have an arrest warrant for obstruction of justice and tampering with evidence for Richard Todd."

"What?" Richard shouted. "Why me?"

Diego removed his phone, pulled up the audio recording, and pushed Play. The sound of a ringback tone came through the speaker, followed by Julia's voice.

"Just breathe," she whispered. "Do what Richard said, and this will work out." She took one calming breath. "You can do this." Julia's breathing suddenly became very choppy, and she started to wail, so when the 911 operator answered, it sounded like Julia was in a genuine panic. They listened as a distraught daughter sniffled and cried her way through the phone call, getting into the pool to check her father for a pulse when the operator instructed her to. She kept up the act until the first responders arrived and the dispatcher disconnected. Silence washed over the room as Richard and Alyssa stared daggers at Julia.

"People don't realize that the 911 recordings begin as soon as your phone connects, and not just when an operator answers," Diego said. "Imagine our surprise when we pulled the recording this morning."

"I can explain," Richard said.

"Don't you say a damn word," Julia snarled.

"Richard, please don't," Alyssa implored.

A shocked hush blanketed the room as Royce read everyone their rights, but the pandemonium resumed when he asked if they understood them. The fur wasn't flying, but accusations were.

"I wish I'd worn a tactical vest with a body cam," Diego called out.

"Ditto." The audio recording would have to be sufficient. Royce stuck two fingers in his mouth and released a sharp whistle that brought the fighting to an immediate halt. "Thank you," he said. "Now, I'm going to start all over again because I need you to verbally acknowledge I've read your rights and that you understand them."

"I want a lawyer!" Alyssa yelled.

"I want a lawyer too, but a different one than hers!" Julia stabbed a finger in her mother's direction.

"It would be a great conflict of interest otherwise." Royce pulled a second pair of cuffs from his back pocket and approached the attorney.

"This isn't a great big conspiracy, Sergeant. You have to believe me," Richard pleaded.

"I'm not the one you need to convince, sir. Let's make this as easy as possible. We'll take the three of you down to the station, book you in, and then you'll be able to phone your attorneys."

The older man's shoulders slumped forward as he accepted his fate. He docilely placed his hands behind his back so Royce could secure them. Diego gently guided Alyssa forward by her upper arms and collected Richard on the way.

"It's going to be okay," the attorney whispered to her.

"I believed you the first time, but I can't anymore." An icy expression formed on Alyssa's features, and she froze out his further attempts to speak to her.

Royce approached Julia and noticed her light eyes darting around the room as if judging her chances for escape. "Don't," he said tersely as his hand hovered near his Taser. "You'll only make your situation worse." Julia narrowed her eyes and studied him intently, as if she could divine his thoughts or willingness to zap her. So he rested his hand on the Taser to prove that he wouldn't hesitate.

"Fine. I'll be out in a matter of hours. You're going to lose your job over this."

Royce let Julia vent her rage and tuned it out, knowing his phone would record every word.

Two hours later, Royce dusted his hands of the entire ordeal. He stopped by the break room to make a bag of popcorn in the microwave and headed downstairs to Sawyer's office. His husband sat at his desk with a pair of readers perched on his nose, sipping from the Hot for Teacher mug Royce had bought him after he agreed to instruct the Explorer cadets. Sawyer glanced up, and an enormous smile spread across his face.

"Is that reaction for me or the popcorn?" Royce asked.

"Both."

Royce stepped into the office and closed the door. He set the treat on the desk and leaned across it to kiss Sawyer firmly on the mouth. His husband chuckled when he pulled back. "What?"

Dark eyes danced with mirth. "Pretty sure our chief was doing a little of that in his office with Beecham before our meeting this morning."

"No way," Royce said. "Tell me."

He munched on popcorn while Sawyer told him about the vibe

he'd picked up on before the conversation they had about Alec Bishop. Groaning, Royce said, "I kinda hoped there wouldn't be any cases that matched so the guy would move on to another city and someone else's husband."

Sawyer tilted his head to the side. "You're not remotely concerned about this guy getting between us, are you?"

Royce considered it for a few seconds too long because Sawyer bounced a popcorn kernel off his head. "I trust you with every fiber of my being. But there's something about this guy that rubs me the wrong way."

Sawyer widened his eyes. "Maybe I should be the one who's worried if he's rubbing on you in any way."

"Hardy har har. You know what I mean. It's that instinct that makes us good cops. I'm not saying the guy doesn't have good intentions, but there are more than a few ways this ordeal could go sideways."

Sawyer nodded. "I have reservations too. I trust Mendoza and Rigby to have all our best interests at heart, and I won't hesitate to step away if necessary." He propped his elbows on the desk and rested his chin on an upturned palm. "Tell me about your day. Did you make a big arrest?"

"Three of them?"

Sawyer pretended to swoon. "Check you out. What happened?"

"Julia clammed up, but Alyssa and Richard Todd sang like canaries."

"So what happened?" Sawyer asked.

"According to them, Julia had overheard enough of the conversation between Jean Claude and Richard to know her father was accused of fathering hundreds of kids through his fertility clinic. She didn't say anything to him about it but quietly seethed with rage. I think she snapped when her father went off on a rampage Saturday morning.

She claimed she only wanted to calm him down. She'd seen her mother's benzodiazepine prescription while snooping in her medicine cabinet and decided they'd do the trick. But he kept bitching, so she kept adding pills, losing track of how many she ground up. The smoothie didn't help and, in fact, made him more irritable. She gave up and just left the house while her mother was getting ready for the mayor's party. When Alyssa finished, she suggested Jean Claude drink some scotch and take a swim. She poured him the first drink and left the house without him. Roughly five hours go by, and Jean Claude doesn't join them, so Julia went home to check on him.

"She freaked out when she found her father in the pool and saw the empty liquor decanter. She called Richard before dialing 911. He left the gathering he'd attended, drove to the mayor's house, and discreetly pulled Alyssa aside without anyone seeing him. Together, they called Julia back, and they quickly realized what had happened. Richard then instructed her to retrieve the prescription bottle from her mother's medicine cabinet to make it look like Jean Claude had intentionally overdosed. It would be an easy leap for law enforcement to make, considering the situation. That's when Richard told us about the conversation he'd had with Jean Claude on Friday afternoon. The doctor denied the allegations, but it was going to be damning to his reputation. A prideful man like him would've hated the scrutiny and negative press, making the overdose more believable." Royce cocked his head to the side. "Richard admitted that he thought their close relationship with the mayor would come in handy, but Barclay supported Rigby's decision to investigate further. If she'd backed down and taken the evidence at face value, we would've probably classified the death as an overdose."

"Do you believe him?" Sawyer asked.

"I believe he's telling the truth as far as he knows it. Did Julia intentionally try to kill her father? I can't say. That will be for DA Babineaux to determine, but I suspect she'll go with the involuntary manslaughter because that's the charge she can prove."

"You did a good job," Sawyer said.

"Sloppy criminals help."

Sawyer shook his head. "So humble."

Royce snorted. "Hardly. I'll swagger around when the situation merits it." He helped himself to another handful of popcorn. "Anything exciting happen around here?"

Sawyer's brown eyes softened, and a serene expression came over his face. Royce only encountered that look when Sawyer slept peacefully or was blissed-out from sex.

"What did you do?"

Sawyer fidgeted with his tie as his lips curved into a sheepish grin. "I called the clinic and talked to Dr. Flores. I just needed…assurances."

Royce arched a brow. "And did you get them?"

"I did. I haven't stopped thinking about what our future is going to look like with our daughter."

"You're so sure we're having a girl."

The smile that lit up Sawyer's face was like nothing Royce had ever seen before. "I am."

"I want to hear all the things you imagined."

Sawyer lowered his hand and waggled his brows. "Let's try to sneak out of here early so I can show you."

CHAPTER FOURTEEN

EVERY MUSCLE IN SAWYER'S BODY ACHED, AND SWEAT RAN DOWN him in rivulets. There were workouts, and then there was Pilates. Christ, how had he ever let Kelsey talk him into taking the class with her? He pulled his foot free from the rope handle and curled up into a fetal ball on the padded board they called a carriage. Sawyer was no stranger to working out. He ran, lifted, and stretched his body at least six days a week and had considered himself to be in excellent shape until Kelsey introduced him to the Pilates Reformer. It was a piece of equipment that looked incredibly basic. He'd scoffed at the simple boxed frame, the padded board on sliders, and the attached pulleys or ropes. Kels had shown him how adjusting the tension springs changed the resistance and intensity of the workout. He cranked the tension up because a fit guy like him could handle it easy peasy, right? Wrong! Sawyer lasted five minutes before he curled into a ball and playfully sucked on his thumb.

"The freaking CIA could add this machine to their interrogation tactics. America's enemies would spill their secrets so fast the agents wouldn't be able to keep up with the information flow."

Kelsey giggled on the machine beside him. "Big baby."

He scowled at his best friend, who looked like a gliding goddess on her carriage. "When you invited me to join you at Pilates, I figured you were trying to get me out of the house so Royce could set up a birthday surprise."

Kelsey glanced his way long enough to roll her eyes. "Your birthday is tomorrow."

"I know, but Sundays are sacred in our house. Royce wouldn't throw a bash and kill our vibe. You must want me dead. It's the only explanation for this abuse."

Kelsey lowered her leg and waited until the carriage stopped before removing her foot from the handle. She bent her elbow and propped her head against her fist. "I brought you here to start your conditioning for fatherhood." They still had seven days before they took their first pregnancy blood test at the clinic, but Kelsey refused to believe the results would be anything but positive.

"Maybe the slight cramping you felt means the IUI wasn't successful and you're going to get your period," Sawyer said.

"Nope, Eeyore. My premenstrual cramps are way more intense. I'm telling you it was implantation cramps. I had them with Ella, and the timing matches." She reached over and took Sawyer's hand. "We read the same material. The sperm would've fertilized the egg within twenty-four hours, but it takes six to twelve days for the egg to attach to the uterine lining. Dr. Flores is going to confirm the pregnancy on Friday. Mark my words."

Giddiness bubbled inside Sawyer, choking out the cautious Gemini twin that he usually let guide his decision-making. The poor guy made a valiant effort to seize control, but the wild child Gemini twin wrapped the Pilates rope around his neck and tightened it until he submitted to the surge of unmitigated joy. "Kels, I'm going to be a dad," he whispered.

"Hell yeah, you are." She pointed at the torture rope attached to the pulley. "Loop your foot back in that handle and get to work. You're going to need more stamina than you can imagine."

Sawyer narrowed his eyes. "For the baby or whatever Royce is planning?"

"Quit pestering me with silly questions about your husband and get to work."

"Because he *is* up to something. Royce asked what time I was leaving and how long I'd be gone. He's setting something up." Sawyer groaned. "I'm too old for parties."

"Just shut up and enjoy whatever he's up to."

"I knew it!" Sawyer exclaimed. "What's the surprise? Give me a hint?"

Kelsey fixed him with a stern look and pointed to the rope handle. "Complete the workout and I'll give you a hint."

Sawyer whined, but it was enough incentive for him to comply. Forty minutes later, it took everything he had to put one foot in front of the other so they could make it to Kelsey's car. Sawyer forgot all about pestering his friend for hints, even after a little dopamine hit from their favorite smoothie shop. He didn't give the surprise another thought until Kels pulled into his driveway. "You owe me a hint."

Kelsey snorted, then picked up her mango smoothie and took a long pull from her straw. She sighed heavily as she returned her drink to the cup holder. "Why are you still here?" She made a shooing motion with her hands.

"It's not a surprise party, is it?"

Kelsey rolled her eyes. "Would I let you walk into an ambush looking like that?"

Sawyer glanced down at his chest and noticed his shirt was still damp with sweat. A quick peek in the rearview mirror showed his wet hair sticking up in clumpy spikes all over. "But you let me go into the smoothie shop looking like this?" He tried to tidy his hair, but his efforts only made things worse.

Kelsey revved the engine to get his attention. "Here's your hint. Your surprise is just for the two of you. Get out and enjoy it."

"Damn, you're kind of mean. Low blood sugar?"

"Pregnancy hormones. Get used to it."

Sawyer removed his seat belt and leaned over the console to kiss her cheek. "I love you. Thanks for showing me how weak I really am."

"You're most welcome, and I love you too. It's amazing what your body will do with a little time and effort."

"I've used that line on Royce a time or two."

Kelsey threw her head back and laughed lustily. "I can't wait to hear all about your surprise."

"That good, huh?"

"It's definitely unique. Andrew will need to step up his game."

With those encouraging remarks, Sawyer grabbed his bag and exited her car. He'd intended to stride to the house with purpose, but he limped like he'd just survived a war. Kelsey rolled down her window and poked her head outside so he could hear her wicked laughter as she drove away. He actually had to stop and massage a cramp in his right calf when he reached the porch. If Royce had energetic sex in mind, he might be disappointed because all Sawyer wanted to do was sprawl on the couch. Dolly and Bones were waiting for him in the foyer when he opened the door. Not unusual, but there was a frantic energy radiating off them that made him a little nervous about what he might find.

"Honey, I'm ho—"

His words died on his lips when he raised his head and saw Royce standing in the center of the living room, wearing white rubber boots that came up to his knees and the pair of pink flamingo booty shorts that barely covered his ass. Sawyer had a similar pair, but they had blue sharks all over them. They'd randomly purchased the shorts and matching bucket hats from a souvenir shop in Put-in-Bay during their honeymoon. Royce looked so ridiculous that it took Sawyer a minute to process what exactly he was seeing.

His husband had moved all the furniture to the edges of the room so that the focal point was the large area rug Royce had given him a thorough fucking on just the previous weekend. Then he noticed a commercial rug shampooer off to the side. It was black, and Royce had taken some kind of white tape or stickers to make it look like Darth Vader. But Royce had taken letter stickers and spelled out Dirt Vader instead. Sawyer suspected the machine was the source of agitation he detected from their pets.

"It's about time you got home." Royce raked his gaze over Sawyer, taking in his sweaty, disheveled condition. "What the hell did they do to you at Pilates?"

Sawyer dropped his bag to the floor and walked into the living room. "Torture. Plain and simple. I have muscles I didn't know existed, and they're weak and pitiful." He stopped when he reached Royce and took his face in both hands. "I fucking love you so much. This is the best birthday surprise ever."

"And I haven't even started my demonstration yet."

Sawyer ran his hand over Royce's bare chest and dipped his fingers beneath his waistband. "This outfit alone is precious. And that damn shampooer is so cute. How much would it cost for us to buy it outright?"

Royce laughed. "You've been hanging around me too long."

"Eternity isn't long enough," Sawyer said before nipping Royce's bottom lip.

"Wow. That torturous exercise has gotten you all randy."

Sawyer shook his head and dropped his hand lower to cup Royce's perfect package. "Nope. I didn't think I had a pulse left until I walked through the door. This is all because of you."

Royce groaned as his eyelids drifted to half-mast. He sucked in a sharp breath and stepped back until Sawyer's hand slipped free from his shorts. "Huh-uh. I put a lot of effort into planning this." He pointed to the couch. "You go lie down and watch."

"Fine, but I might get my dick out."

Royce swayed a bit, and Sawyer could see the conflict brewing in his eyes. "Fine, but it will be all your fault if I ruin the rug because you distracted me."

Sawyer shrugged. "We'll buy a new one, even though this rug is practically new since we just had it professionally cleaned."

Royce narrowed his eyes. "Is that when the fetish began?"

"Not this again." Sawyer flopped onto the couch. "Ready for my show."

And what a performance it was. Royce did such a good job that Sawyer conked out after only a few passes over the rug. He didn't know how long he'd slept, but he woke with dried drool on the corner of his mouth and a crick in his neck. Sawyer struggled to remember why he was on the couch and retraced his day, starting with the torture class called Pilates. He'd gotten a smoothie with Kelsey and had come home to a surprise. His eyes widened when he recalled Royce in his shorty shorts and white rubber boots. Sawyer jackknifed off the couch and groaned when some of his muscle groups spasmed in protest at the sudden movement.

He bit back a moan as he searched the empty living room. Other parts started to come alive besides the ones that ached, namely his senses. A tantalizing aroma of butter, garlic, cheese, and shrimp tickled his nose and made his stomach rumble. Sawyer followed the smells like a bloodhound to find a sight more delicious than the food cooking on the stove. Royce still wore the shorty shorts and rubber boots as he stirred a pan of what Sawyer knew would be cheesy grits to go with the shrimp. The delicious meal was one of Royce's culinary masterpieces, and his other crowning glory rested on a cooling rack.

"Feel better after your nap?" Royce asked.

Sawyer answered with a savage grunt as he shuffled his exhausted legs over to the island to peer into the mixing bowl next to the richest, most delicious chocolate cake he'd ever tasted. The recipe belonged to Royce's mother, and he only baked the cake for special occasions. The decadent fudgy icing was ready and just sitting in the bowl, waiting for someone to do a quality check. *Don't mind if I do.* He dipped his forefinger toward the bowl, but Royce yanked it away before he could make contact with the heavenly treat.

"Hey," Sawyer said with a pout. "It's my birthday."

"Wash your hands first. I don't know where they've been."

"Torture," Sawyer said as he ambled toward the sink. "I've never sweated so much in my life." He became aware of how stiff his workout clothes were. "Ew, I'm so gross."

Royce tsked. "And you wanted to dip those nasty digits in my icing."

Sawyer waggled his brow. "I love your icing." He dried his hands and rounded the island to kiss Royce. "I'm sorry I fell asleep and ruined your surprise."

"I don't have to take the carpet cleaner back until Monday. We've got plenty of time for more demonstrations." Royce kissed him but crinkled his nose when he pulled back.

"God, do I stink?"

"You smell like you've had a really good workout. Why don't you go take a shower while I finish dinner."

"Dinner?" Sawyer asked. "Have I been out that long?"

"I've never heard you snore so loud. You drowned out the noise of the machine. Dolly and Bones were more afraid of you than it."

Sawyer scrubbed a hand over his face. "How about putting this food in the warming drawer so you can join me in the shower?"

"Even exhausted, you're the smartest man I know."

Sawyer stole a few bites of shrimp and grits before they stowed the food safely away from the pets. The baking rack with the cake halves went back into the cool oven, and Royce put the icing in the refrigerator so Bones wouldn't help himself to Sawyer's birthday treat. Royce took his hand and led him from the kitchen. Sawyer moaned and grumbled his way to the bathroom and rested against the vanity while Royce started the shower.

"That must've been some class," Royce said. "You're in the best shape of anyone I know."

"It was evil. There's no way I'll ever do it again."

Once they stepped beneath the hot spray, the only ache he worried about was the one between his legs. Royce dropped to his knees and took Sawyer in his mouth, working his erection with an expertise earned from lots of practice. But his loving ministrations turned almost cruel when he drew Sawyer's release beyond his breaking point.

"Let me come. It's my birthday."

Royce's chuckle rumbled along the length of Sawyer's dick and vibrated his balls. He tightened his mouth around Sawyer's shaft, sucked hard, and slowly eased back until his erection sprang free.

Sawyer grunted as his balls drew tight. "You told me not to come without you."

"Your birthday isn't until tomorrow." Royce circled his finger in the air, telling Sawyer to turn around. His feet slipped in soapy suds as he eagerly complied. "Careful. We sure as hell don't want to end up at the hospital after a slip and fall. Brace your arms against the tile." Royce spread his ass cheeks apart and buried his face between them before Sawyer could respond or comply.

Sawyer cried out and braced his forearms against the cool tile when Royce used his tongue to arouse him further and open Sawyer's pucker. He hung his head and watched his throbbing dick jerk from the intensity of the stimulation. "I won't last."

Royce responded by sinking his teeth in his ass cheek. "You will."

Eventually, his wicked husband kissed a path up his back before taking him fast and furiously up against the shower wall. The tight enclosure amplified their moans of pleasure and jubilant cries when they came. Sawyer clung to Royce like a life raft once he regained enough strength in his legs to turn in his husband's embrace.

"Best. Birthday. Ever."

Royce laughed and kissed his temple. "We're just getting started, baby."

Sawyer was too tired to lift his head from Royce's shoulder. "What's next?"

Royce's hand landed with a wet *thwack* against his ass cheek. "Birthday spankings."

EPILOGUE

SAWYER STOOD UP AND PACED ACROSS THE ROOM, HOPING IT would ease his nervous energy. If he sat any longer, his bouncing knees would've vibrated his chair across the room. He stared at a wall of photos featuring the success stories of former patients at the clinics. Photos, ultrasounds, testimonials, and thank-you cards covered nearly every inch of the huge corkboard, but there was a gap on the bottom left corner for another success story. Theirs?

Kelsey's blood draw to test for the presence of hCG had occurred at eight that morning, but they had to wait a few hours for the clinic's in-house lab to process the results. They'd gone to breakfast, where Kelsey and Royce calmly chatted about everyday things while eating pancakes, sausage, and scrambled eggs. He'd barely picked at his egg white omelet, which he regretted when his stomach released an angry growl two hours later as they waited for Dr. Flores to give their results.

"That sounded painful," Royce said as he moved in behind him to wrap strong arms around Sawyer's waist. "We're going to have things to contribute to the board soon."

He turned in Royce's embrace and kissed him briefly. "We are."

A wrapper rattled across the room, and Kelsey extended a protein bar she pulled from her purse. "I came prepared."

He returned to his chair beside her and accepted the offering with a grateful thanks. "Which one of us is going to haul around a big-ass purse everywhere?" Sawyer asked before taking a bite. "The baby will have a ton of stuff, and we're going to need snacks."

"It's called a diaper bag, and we'll take turns carrying it," Royce said. "Evangeline has probably already set her eyes on a Louis Vuitton or something."

"One of those would cost more than the high-end stroller you've been drooling over," Kelsey told Royce. His husband had wasted no time in adding a ton of stuff to the Pinterest board.

"What's high-end about a stroller?" Sawyer asked.

Royce sat beside Sawyer and crossed his arms over his chest in a defensive posture. "It's made with a sturdier metal frame for stability."

"The little protective cloth awning cost four hundred dollars alone," Kelsey said. "Massive thing. That stroller will weigh a ton."

"But our girl will be safe," Royce said.

Sawyer melted on the spot and decided they'd buy the expensive stroller.

Royce flexed his arms so his biceps strained against his shirt. "We've got plenty of muscle."

"Join us at Pilates on Saturday," Kelsey said with a wicked gleam in her eyes.

Sawyer was doubting his agreement to return to the studio when a soft knock sounded at the door. His breath caught in his lungs, and he couldn't have talked if he'd wanted to. Dr. Flores opened the door and stepped inside, but Sawyer couldn't tell by her expression if she had good or bad news. He reached for Kelsey's hand with his right and Royce's hand with his left. Dr. Flores' mouth curved into a big smile, and the three of them cheered before she could say the words. She waited patiently for them to hug and celebrate the positive results.

"Congratulations," she said once they wound down. "Your hCG levels are exactly where we want them to be. We'll have you come back periodically for new draws to make sure the levels increase the way they should. You've already started prenatal vitamins well before we started this process, so it's just a waiting game for a bit. I'll do an ultrasound to confirm the viability in six weeks, and I'll turn you over to your ob-gyn after that. Do any of you have questions for me right now?"

Sawyer looked at Royce, who had a matching set of tear trails on his face. He cleared his throat to speak. "Do you have questions for her?"

Royce swallowed hard and faced Dr. Flores. "Do you accept hugs?"

She laughed and opened her arms. "Bring it in."

Sawyer, Kelsey, and Royce gathered Dr. Flores into a group hug before they turned her loose. Kelsey stopped at the counter on their way out to schedule her follow-up blood tests before the trio strolled into the sunlight.

"Are you guys going back to work?" Kelsey asked.

"We took the day off," Sawyer said. "We knew there was no way we'd be able to concentrate."

Kelsey giggled and shook her head. "I'm not going back to work either."

Sawyer ran his hand through his hair. "How are we supposed to keep this news to ourselves for like ten more weeks? I feel like I'm going to burst."

"Maybe tell the people closest to you," Kelsey suggested.

"My closest people already know," Royce said, gesturing to her and Sawyer. "I can think of an activity that will help Sawyer work through his excess energy."

"Yeah, I hear you're good for that," Kelsey teased.

"Not that." Royce tilted his head. "Well, not yet, anyway. Let's paint the nursery. Kelsey can float around the pool like a water goddess and maybe boss us around."

Kelsey hitched her purse higher on her shoulder and strode to her car. "Damn, I'm loving this idea. I'll meet you there."

Royce watched her walk away, and Sawyer took advantage of the distraction to send the Maury Povich GIF he'd found on the internet. It showed the talk show host holding up a manilla envelope with paternity results and the words, "You are the father," flashing across the bottom. He tucked his phone away so he could watch Royce's face when he opened the text. "Who's bugging me?" Royce saw the sender, then quirked his brow at Sawyer.

"Just open it."

Royce tapped his phone and watched the GIF play on repeat for a few seconds. He snapped his head up and met Sawyer's gaze, a big smile on his face. "I'm the father."

"Hell yeah, you are."

"I'm the father!" Royce's shout startled an elderly lady going into the medical building next door. "Sorry, ma'am." He turned back to Sawyer with a look of pure wonder on his face. "We're going to have a baby," he whispered.

"We are." Sawyer would never forget the moment in the clinic when Royce offered to give him the one thing he wanted most in the world: his baby.

"Whose last name will we give her? We can't do a hyphenated double-barreled last name. Can you imagine? Key-Locke. Locke-Key. I refuse to be one of those parents who set their kids up for relentless bullying."

Sawyer hooked his finger through Royce's belt loop and tugged him forward. "I'm already one step ahead of you." He reached into his back pocket and pulled out his wallet. "I have a surprise for you. It's a little something I worked on this week."

"My birthday isn't until October."

"Father's Day is next weekend." Sawyer pulled his driver's license from the clear plastic slot and handed it to him.

Royce stared at it for the longest time before lifting his head. Joy shimmered in those pale gray eyes he loved so damn much. "Sawyer Locke."

"I changed my name to Locke legally, though I'll continue to use Key professionally. I checked with HR, and they said it—"

Royce smashed his lips against Sawyer's right there on the side-walk. "Fuck. You went and did it."

Sawyer chuckled. "Surprised you?"

"Yeah, that too," Royce said. "But I didn't think I could love you more." He held up Sawyer's new license. "I was so wrong."

To be continued in…
The Sinner's Son on September 9, 2025.
You can preorder now here:

and…

Brokered Betrayals on December 16, 2025.
You can preorder now here:

Staying in touch is easier than ever and prettier too! Would you like to follow me on all the socials, signup for my newsletter, or join my Facebook reader's group? You can do all those things by checking out this handy hub on my website @ www.aimeenicolewalker.com/links.

OTHER BOOKS BY
AIMEE NICOLE WALKER

Curl Up and Dye Mysteries
Dyeing to be Loved
Something to Dye For
Dyed and Gone to Heaven
I Do, or Dye Trying
A Dye Hard Holiday
Ride or Dye
Curl Up and Dye Box Set

Road to Blissville Series
Unscripted Love
Someone to Call My Own
Nobody's Prince Charming
This Time Around
Smoke in the Mirror
Inside Out
Prescription for Love

Welcome to Blissville Collection (Both M/M Blissville series)
Volume One
Volume Two

The Lady is Mine Series
The Lady is a Thief
The Lady Stole My Heart

Queen City Rogue Series

Broken Halos
Wicked Games
Beautiful Trauma

Zero Hour Series

Ground Zero
Devil's Hour
Zero Divergence
Zero Hour Box Set

Sawyer and Royce: Matrimony and Mayhem

The Magnolia Murders
Marriage is Murder
Killer Honeymoon

Sinister in Savannah Series

Ride the Lightning
Mr. Perfect
Pretty Poison
Sinister in Savannah Box Set

Savannah Universe Standalone Books

Invisible Strings
Bad at Love
About Last Night
Just Say When
Single in Savannah Box Set

Standalone Novels

Second Wind

ACKNOWLEDGMENTS

Many, many thanks to Charity, Sandra, and Lori for your editing services and for keeping me in line. These ladies are consummate professionals and are pure joy to work with. And much love to Natasha Snow and Wander Aguiar for this gorgeous cover and to Stacey Ryan Blake for her stunning interior designs. All of you make my books sparkle and shine so beautifully—inside and out. I thank my lucky stars that I get to work with such wonderfully talented people.

Sending much love to Melinda James Rueter and Racheal Yunk for bravely reading my rough drafts and providing priceless feedback. And I don't know where I'd be without CC Belle, my amazing personal assistant, who brings organization and so much joy into my life. Love you, ladies!

xoxo
Aimee

ABOUT
AIMEE NICOLE WALKER

Aimee Nicole Walker is an international bestselling author of Male/Male contemporary romance and romantic suspense novels. Her stories guarantee hunks with big...hearts, lots of humor and heat, and the occasional homicide. Aimee is a lifelong dreamer, an avid reader, and an off-key singer. Only two of those traits help her craft captivating characters and charming communities where everyone is welcome. She uses the other quirk to entertain her pets during writing breaks.

Aimee has loved the same guy for over thirty years. Her husband is the reason she can write romance novels, and he's possibly inspired a fictional murder plot a time or ten. They share three adult children, two adorable grandsons, and a menagerie of pets that don't include goats or donkeys...yet. Love inspires everything she does, books keep her sane, and coffee is the magic elixir that fuels her day.

Let's stay in touch!

Would you like to learn more about my work, sign up for my newsletter, or follow my social media accounts?
Here's your fast pass to all things Aimee:

www.ingramcontent.com/pod-product-compliance
Lightning Source LLC
Chambersburg PA
CBHW031419250626
47155CB00004B/1547